Presented to

**Clear Lake City - County
Freeman Branch Library**

By

**Friends of the Freeman Library**

. Harris County
    **Public Library**
        your pathway to knowledge

ANNIE'S ATTIC MYSTERIES™

# Rag Doll
### in the Attic

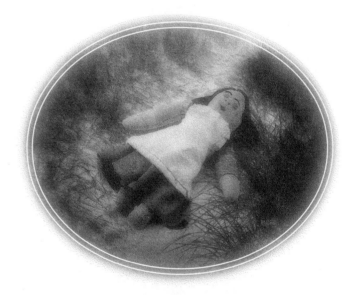

## Jan Fields

AnniesMysteries.com

Library of Congress-in-Publication Data
Rag Doll in the Attic / by Jan Fields
p. cm.
ISBN: 978-1-59635-339-8
I. Title
                                    2010916180

AnniesMysteries.com
800-282-6643
Annie's Attic Mysteries™
Series Creator: Stenhouse & Associates, Ridgefield, Connecticut
Series Editors: Ken and Janice Tate
Art Director: Brad Snow
Production Artist: Nicole Gage

10  11  12  13  14  |  Printed in China  |  10 9 8 7 6 5 4 3 2

# Dedication

For my mother, who taught me my
love of needlework and mysteries.

# ~ 1 ~

*The calendar claims it's still summer in Maine, but a cold wind blows up from the water and tosses the hair of the three young girls hurrying along the dirt road. The tallest of the three pushes strands of her dark bob behind her ears and laughs. The girl beside her is fair and wears her longer hair in a high ponytail that defies the tugging of the wind. She's so much shorter than her long-legged friend that she has to skip to keep up.*

*A younger girl with long, dark braids lags behind, gripping a doll in her arms, though many would think her too old for dolls. She glances to the left, where the woods form a wall of black that eventually falls away onto the beach. She shivers from cold tinged with fear. Anything could lurk in the woods. "I'm cold," she shouts.*

*The girls' skirts flap around their legs as the rough road grows steeper. The lead girl turns and calls out, "Come on, slowpoke. This was your idea."*

*The other girl grips the doll still tighter and mutters, "Was not." Her words are snatched away by the wind almost as soon as they leave her mouth.*

*"Don't tease," the blonde scolds, giving her friend a gentle shove. She turns a sunny smile to the frightened girl. "Come up here. I'll hold your hand."*

*"I'm fine," the third says with a scowl. "I'm not a baby."*

7

The three reach a narrowing in the road where the cliff side to their right is deeply eroded from the wind and water. The wind slips between the rocks of the cliff with an eerie howl. "Sounds like the ghosts are calling you, Jenny," the leader says, laughing again.

The girl in the rear stomps forward then, pushing between them. "There's no such thing as ghosts," she says. "There's no point trying to scare me, Jo."

"No point," Jo agrees. "You're doing well enough on your own."

The younger girl sniffs. "I just don't like being out when a storm is coming." She looks up into the dark night. "We're going to get soaked. Mother won't like seeing your new dress get ruined. You were supposed to save it for school."

Jo shrugs. "I didn't want to save it for school; that's boring. What fun is something new if you can't wear it?" She skips ahead and spins to make her skirt swirl. "Besides, a little water won't hurt it."

"Don't fight. We're almost there," the blond girl says, pointing ahead as they crest the next hill. A dark hulk looms. When they crane their necks back to try and see the top, they spot the wide, white light sweeping the sky from the top of the building. They have almost reached the lighthouse.

Just then, lightning splits the sky into jagged shards, showing off the weathered clapboards of the lighthouse keeper's cottage. An old dog with a huge, square head staggers to his feet on the porch and stares at them in that instant before darkness swoops back in.

The girl with the doll backs up a bit. "If the dog barks, that'll bring the old man out. He'll call the sheriff."

*"Only if he sees us," Jo says. "We just touch the lighthouse tower and run. No one's going to catch us. Tell me, little sister, are you a Wild Jay or a chicken?"*

*Another crack of lightning strikes, and it seems to split open the skies. Rain pounds down on the three girls, soaking them in an instant. The torrent weighs them down and turns the road into a muddy mess that catches at their feet. The very air is so full of water, it's hard to breathe. It presses down on their chests making them gasp ...*

Annie Dawson struggled to wake up, as the weight on her chest seemed to grow heavier. She blinked in the morning sunshine and reached up to her chest, alarmed. Her hands brushed soft fur. "Boots," she gasped, pushing the cat off onto the other side of the bed.

She frowned at the cat. Boots looked back at her and blinked in innocent reproof. Annie could almost imagine the chubby cat asking, "Why did you push me?"

"Don't bother looking innocent," Annie said, though a laugh bubbled up as the cat began licking her small white paw. "I know that was some trick to get breakfast sooner."

"Me-rrrow?" Boot inquired, and Annie laughed again. She secretly suspected Boots understood all English words related to food.

Annie slipped her feet into the pale blue slippers that lay neatly beside the bed. She tried to remember what she'd been dreaming about, but only the last horrible feeling of near suffocation stayed with her. Somehow she didn't think it was a very pleasant dream.

"Indecision is giving me nightmares," she said aloud as

she stood and reached for the soft floral-print flannel robe that lay over the beautiful oak rocker near the foot of the bed. Annie held it against her cheek for just a moment, remembering the smile on Wayne's face when she'd opened the shiny white gift box that held it.

Even after LeeAnn was grown and moved out, Wayne had insisted on giving her a Mother's Day gift each year. "For being the best mother our daughter could have," he always said.

Annie blinked away tears and slipped into the robe. She wondered if she'd ever be able to visit those sweet memories of Wayne without crying. She looked around the bedroom at the mix of her things and the beautiful things her grandmother, Betsy Holden, had left behind. The room reminded her of her own situation—they were both in transition.

Annie walked down the stairs and into the front room. She opened the door, breathing the sweet scent of lilacs wafting in from the two shrubs in the front yard. Spring had settled in, and it was well past time for her to decide what to do about Grey Gables. It seemed she'd been making the firm decision to make the decision ever since she'd gotten here.

The snows of winter had made her almost certain that the right answer was to rush back to the Texas warmth. But then New England threw her a new surprise, and she fell in love with Maine in springtime. Early in the spring, she'd watched the soil eagerly to see what spring bulbs Gram had in the beds, like a kid waiting for Christmas. The burst of yellow daffodil trumpets had long ago given way to irises and shy lily of the valley. It was so beautiful here, but should she stay?

Annie tried to imagine what her grandmother would

suggest if she were still here in her beautiful old house. Then Annie sighed, Betsy Holden had not had a wishy-washy bone in her whole body. She would give Annie a gentle shake and tell her to follow her heart and do it soon!

"I did make one decision," she said as Boots twined through her legs. "I decided to go back for the twins' birthday party." Annie paused a moment, hoping that talking to herself didn't really mean she was turning into a crazy, old cat lady. Then she sighed and turned to walk to the kitchen, keeping a careful eye on Boots, who often seemed to consider tripping Annie to be the ultimate kitty game.

She fetched the carafe from the coffeemaker and filled it at the sink. At least the grandchildren's birthday party gave her a deadline. If she hadn't made a decision by the time she went home to Texas for the party, she'd never get away. Her daughter, LeeAnn, had made it plain as paint that she wanted her mother back in Texas, immediately if not sooner. Annie had to admit, there was a certain temptation to simply let the decision be taken out of her hands.

Boots meowed at Annie's feet to remind her that the cat was near starvation.

"You forget," Annie said, pointing. "I'm the one who woke up in the middle of suffocation by cat. I know exactly how fat you are."

Boots stalked over to her bowl and flopped down with a muted thump, giving Annie a rude glance every now and then.

Just as Annie finished pouring food in the cat's bowl, she heard a knock at the door. She looked down at her softly faded robe, and then peeked around the corner of the kitchen entry. Her dear friend Alice MacFarlane stood at the front screen door carrying something wrapped in embroidered tea towels. Annie's stomach growled at the thought of tasting some more of Alice's wonderful baking.

"Did we have breakfast plans?" Annie asked as she hurried over and pulled open the door.

"No, but I tried out a new coffee-cake recipe, and I want to test it on you before I decide to make one for my next Divine Décor party."

Alice was constantly trying out new baking recipes, both to enchant her clients and as a way to work off some of her nervous energy. Alice slipped by Annie and headed for the kitchen.

"So I'm your lab rat again?" Annie asked, laughing.

Alice grinned back over her shoulder. "Will it help if I promise you'll be a very happy lab rat?"

"That does help." Annie poured coffee into thick green mugs for the two of them as Alice collected two of Gram's Aster Blue plates. They settled down at the kitchen table, and Annie smiled, thinking of how much she'd grown to enjoy reconnecting with Alice after so many years apart. Even though so much had happened to them, the years just seemed to fall away when they got together.

Alice cut generous squares of the coffee cake she'd brought. "This is cranberry-pecan upside-down coffee cake," she said. "It's full of brown sugar and butter and other things we shouldn't even consider eating."

"Sounds like another Alice MacFarlane baking success story," Annie said, breathing in the sweet scent as she set coffee mugs on the table.

"So, why are you still in your jammies?" Alice asked.

"You're usually such an early bird."

"I didn't sleep well last night," Annie said. "Nightmares." She slipped into her chair and picked a candied pecan from the top of her slice of cake and popped it into her mouth. "And I woke up under a subtle attack from Boots."

"A cat attack could give anyone nightmares," Alice said, smiling at the gray cat who sat with her back to them, washing up after her breakfast with the single-minded focus that only a cat can manage. "What was the dream about?"

Annie frowned and peered into her mug, trying to remember. "I don't remember much. It was dark. I think there were children in it." She shook her head. "I'm wondering if maybe the children in my dream represent my grandchildren. Their birthday is coming up, and I'm probably nervous about going back to Brookfield for the party. All this indecision about the future is probably giving me nightmares."

"Well, we can solve that," Alice said with a mischievous grin. "You just decide once and for all to call Stony Point your home. How easy was that?"

Annie shook her head. "I wish it were so simple."

"It's only as hard as you make it," Alice said, echoing something Betsy Holden had told each of them many times when they were young girls.

"Right, Gram," Annie said wryly as she stood to clear the small kitchen table. Annie and Alice chatted a bit longer before Alice left to let Annie get dressed.

"I'll see you at A Stitch in Time," Alice said, her blue eyes sparkling, as she pushed open the front screen door. "You can tell everyone about your nightmares. We'll call it the new mystery. You know they'll love it."

"No mysteries!" Annie shook a finger at Alice, laughing. "We'll just have to enjoy the needlework and the chatting. I am completely mystery free."

"Sure you are," Alice said as she slipped out the door. "For now."

Annie shook her head, still smiling as she walked upstairs to her room to slip into something a little less comfortable for the rest of her day.

# ~ 2 ~

A stiff breeze made the flag snap over Annie's head as she walked across the Town Square, enjoying the scent of freshly mowed grass and the stubbly feel of it under her feet. The sun was warm on her face, but the breeze made her glad she'd added a cotton sweater over her cheery floral sundress. She'd dressed up, hoping to chase away any lingering effects of her poor sleep.

She paused to watch a redheaded boy in a Stony Point T-shirt chase a little girl with the same flame-colored hair as his. They circled the flagpole as the girl shrieked with laughter. The burst of warmth had brought out a few early tourists, hoping to catch some of the slower life of a small town before the huge summer rush.

Annie smiled as the sound of the children reminded her of her grandchildren. John had the same love of teasing and chasing his sister Joanna. It would be great to see LeeAnn, Herb, and the twins again for the party.

As Annie crossed the street and headed up the sidewalk to A Stitch in Time, the breeze blew a strand of hair across her face. She tucked it behind one ear, and then paused. Something about the gesture felt so familiar. She'd seen someone do it recently, and her mind nudged her, urging her to catch hold of the memory. She stood, trying to relax and let it come to her, but it danced just at the edge of real remembering.

*They say the memory is the first thing to go,* Annie thought with a slight smile. She looked back toward the Town Square, marveling at how much this felt like her town now. She had come to love the bustle of the tourists and the warm smiles of the locals. Then, when the snow moved in and drove the tourists home again, it had felt even cozier, even more like home. Was it time to declare that Stony Point was where she belonged?

Then she thought of the house she'd shared with Wayne in Texas. In her mind, she counted off the reasons she couldn't let it go: There was the tree they'd planted the year LeeAnn was born, so they could watch it grow with her. And then there were the shelves Wayne had built for her just before he declared that he would never become a master carpenter. He was a gifted salesman, but not nearly as good at working with his hands.

For a second, Annie's eyes filled again as she pictured his hands. Nothing had ever felt more right than holding his hand as they walked together. Nothing was ever more beautiful than the sight of his hands holding their baby daughter. She couldn't just sell the house she'd shared with him for so many years.

Go? Stay? Sometimes she seemed no closer to a decision than the day she'd arrived. Stony Point felt more and more like home, but a piece of her heart would always lay in that house in Texas. The thought of selling it to strangers and never walking down the halls again made her stomach twist with grief. Could she face never running her fingers along the pencil lines that marked LeeAnn's growing years on the trim of her closet door? She pictured a new family painting over the marks, feeling nothing about them. She couldn't just let that happen, could she?

Annie sighed with the sheer impossibility of the decision. "Eternal transition," she muttered.

"Sounds like a good name for a band," a deep voice said from slightly behind her. "Or a beach song."

Annie turned to face the handsome mayor of Stony Point, Ian Butler. Her face grew warm at the realization that he'd caught her talking to herself. Ian peered at her for a moment and said, "Is something wrong, Annie? You seem upset."

"I'm fine," she said, smiling sheepishly. "You just caught me woolgathering, as Gram would say."

"You wouldn't be working out a new mystery, would you?" he asked.

Annie laughed. "Only the eternal mystery of what I want."

Ian held up his hands and laughed. "I was never any good at guessing what a woman wants. I'd be no help there."

"That's OK. Moral support is good too."

"You always have that," he assured her; then he gestured up the street. "Want to grab a coffee with me at The Cup & Saucer?"

"That sounds great, but I'm late for a meeting of the Hook and Needle Club." Annie held up her bag of wool. "I'm in serious need of help with my latest project."

"You forget," he countered. "I've seen the baby blankets you've made for auctions and such since you came here. I can't imagine you needing much help. They looked great to me, even if the only baby I have is Tartan."

"Well, at least you won't wake up with a schnauzer sitting

on your chest," Annie said. "I think Boots may be out to get me."

Ian laughed. "I sometimes suspect that about Tartan when he decides he needs an extra walk on those icy days in the middle of January. At least *you* don't have to walk a cat in the snow."

Annie pictured Ian as she'd seen him several times during the colder season, decked out in a parka over a woolly fisherman's sweater and work boots. The icy chill of Stony Point had certainly been a big change from Texas winters where it was a rare day when you needed more than a light sweater.

She found she liked the extremes of temperature, as long as she had a cozy room at Gram's to head home to. "So far, Boots only asks for food," she said, pulling herself back to the here and now. "But she does ask for it often."

"Are you sure I can't lure you away for coffee and a rousing game of who has the most difficult pet? I'll spot you ten points for the litter box. I really don't ever want to be around a litter box." His smile was teasing as he folded his arms across his chest.

"Sounds like fun, but I really do have to run. This project is a new one for me. Since I made it through the sweater I crocheted for myself in the fall, I've let Kate talk me into something totally over my head. It's all lace and beads. I know Joanna will love it, if I don't end up with a big snarly mess." She took a calming breath as she realized she might be stressing out the tiniest bit over the sweater. She patted Ian's arm. "I'll take a rain check on the coffee."

Ian agreed with a smile, and Annie hurried down the street. She hoped she wasn't being selfish to ask Kate to concentrate on *her* project during the meeting. Kate Stevens worked at A Stitch in Time and made some of the most fantastic crocheted clothing that Annie had ever seen. She had suggested all the embellishments and extra details for this ambitious birthday present for Joanna.

Annie peeked through the wide storefront window, just below the stenciled store name: *A Stitch in Time*. She saw the circle of overstuffed armchairs were nearly full. Everyone had gotten to the meeting before her.

Annie pulled open the frosted-glass door, hearing the tinkle of the small bell that rang constantly throughout the summer and could be counted on to ring now and then during their meetings. The needlecraft shop was very popular with tourists and locals alike, both because it had a beautiful selection of yarns and fabrics, and because the owner Mary Beth Brock was as warm and friendly as she was shrewd about business. The gorgeous crocheted clothes on mannequins all over the shop, designed and made by Kate, didn't hurt business either. Annie suspected that one of the smartest business decisions Mary Beth had made was hiring the talented young woman as an assistant.

"Sorry I'm late," Annie said as she hurried to the empty chair next to Kate.

"You're only late if you don't come at all," Peggy Carson said, looking up from the small book cover she was quilting. Peggy had told them at the last meeting that her little girl, Emily, had asked for her own diary, and Peggy wanted to make a very personal one, so she'd started the darling pink cover to slip over a blank notebook. Alice was surprised to see Peggy had already done so much. Peggy's projects were notoriously slow, and she was often late for meetings as she had to slip them into her breaks at The Cup & Saucer where she worked long hours. Yet none of that seemed to dull the young woman's cheerful curiosity. "Alice tells us you have a new mystery."

Annie blinked and looked across at her friend. "I do?"

"The mystery of the mashing cat," Alice intoned in an ominous voice, then giggled. "Unless it's the mystery of the fuzzy nightmare."

The group laughed and even the normally austere Stella Brickson looked up from her knitting and allowed a small smile to slip across her patrician face. "I don't think Boots counts as a mystery," Annie said. "I'm mystery free unless you count the mystery of how I'll get this jacket done in time for the twins' birthday party. This has to be the scariest project I've ever worked on."

"I don't know," Gwendolyn Palmer said, her blue eyes sparkling with mischief. "You've jumped into some pretty scary projects since you came back to Stony Point."

Annie nodded. "OK, scariest crochet project."

Kate leaned closer to look at the stitches in the rose-colored jacket front. "You've done very well," she said. "You're almost to the part where you'll begin working in the beads."

"And that's why I need you," Annie said. "I'm not sure how to handle the stitch tension as I work in the beads. I'm definitely never going to be able to compete with the gorgeous clothes you make. I'm terrified of messing this up."

"You just don't give yourself enough credit," Kate said, and she walked Annie through the first row of beading.

The group worked on their different projects with only

occasional conversation for nearly half an hour. A small group of women came in, and Mary Beth jumped up to wait on them since Kate was tied up with helping Annie. Finally, Mary Beth settled back in her seat. "Actually, I know a mystery," she said with her pixie-like smile. "And I'd love to hear the answer, Annie."

Annie looked up. "What's that?"

"Are you going to be coming back to us after the birthday party?" Mary Beth asked. Annie noticed that all of the women had stopped their work to look at Annie avidly. Apparently this was a question that every member of the Hook and Needle Club—including Annie—had on her mind.

"I don't know," Annie sighed. "I want to. I'm sure I will, but then I think about Texas and LeeAnn and the kids ... and I'm back to not knowing."

As she finished speaking, the bell tinkled over the door again and Mary Beth jumped up. This time, they all recognized the blond woman who stepped through the door and pushed her oversized glasses up on her nose nervously as she looked at the group. Valerie Duffy was one of the librarians from the Stony Point Public Library. "I'm sorry for interrupting your meeting," she said, looking around the daunting ring of women in the overstuffed chairs.

"It's not a problem, Valerie." Mary Beth's bright smile could make anyone feel at home. "I didn't know you did needlecrafts."

"I don't," Valerie said. "That's why I was hoping you ladies could help me. I've been running around trying to do two jobs since our children's librarian retired."

Even Stella laid down her knitting to look at Valerie

with interest, and Mary Beth nodded. "If this is about the summer reading program, I would be glad to do a small craft program with the kids. We had fun with them last year, and they seemed to enjoy the bookmarks we made."

Valerie smiled. "I'm glad. I was hoping you would. But I have a little bigger favor to ask." She pulled a large doll from her satchel. "We're having a writing contest this year and giving prizes to the winners. For the girl prize on the elementary level, we were planning to buy a doll that tied into some kind of book theme, but the library budget is a bit tight this year." She paused. "I was hoping you or the ladies in your group could make a book-themed outfit for this doll? Then we could give it as a prize."

"Oh, that sounds like fun," Kate said, jumping up from her chair and hurrying over to look at the doll. She ran her hand over the doll's long dark hair. "I made doll clothes for Vanessa's dolls until she grew too old to appreciate them anymore."

"That's just wonderful," Valerie said, relief clear on her face. "I know you'll do something a little girl would love. Oh, I almost forgot. I have one more favor!"

"Let me guess," Alice said. "Cross-stitch bookmarks for all the kids?"

Peggy laughed and joined in. "No, I bet it's quilted book covers."

Stella waved a hand at the younger women, though her eyes were twinkling. As the matriarch of their group, she often felt the need to tone down any excessive high spirits. "Maybe we should let Valerie tell us."

"Nothing so big," Valerie assured them. "I'm planning

a display of old toys for the big glass case in the children's room. I'm asking everyone to check their attics and storage to see if they have anything they could lend us for the display."

Annie and Alice looked at each other. "Gram's tea set would be perfect," Annie said.

"Back to the attic!" Alice announced.

"That's wonderful," Valerie said, smiling at each of them. "Attics can just be a gold mine, can't they?"

She looked surprised as all the women of the Hook and Needle Club laughed.

# — 3 —

Rain soaks the three young girls to the skin in seconds, turning their skirts into sodden rags that cling to their legs. The wind turns from cold to icy in an instant. The girl with the doll clutched to her chest stumbles backward down the road, blinking at the rain falling into her eyes from her fringe of bangs. "This is stupid," she says, gasping from the cold. "I just want to go home, Jo!"

"We're almost there," the tall girl answers, her long forward strides turning into a trudge through mud. "If we don't touch the lighthouse, we came all this way for nothing. Come on, Jenny, don't chicken out now."

"I'm not chicken," Jenny shouts.

The third girl's light hair clings to her face, darkened by the rain. She tugs on her tall friend's arm. "This isn't fun anymore. I think we should just go home."

"Look, it's right there," Jo says, pointing off into the darkness. "Right there. Let's just do it." She turns angrily and stomps toward the lighthouse. "I'm not going back to school and admit that we were too chicken to touch a wall. You guys have to decide if you want the Wild Jays to be a legend or a joke."

The blond girl smiles slightly at the younger. "You wait here," she says kindly. "It'll be fine. We'll run up and touch it. That will count for all three of us."

*"I don't care about what counts anymore,"* the younger girl says. *"We shouldn't have come."*

*The blonde pats her arm, and then turns and races up the hill. As she passes the porch, she hears the jingle of dog tags. The lighthouse keeper's dog is following her, she can hear the tags jingling closer and closer. The jingling seems so loud ...*

Annie woke with a start as the jingling of the dog tags became the ringing of the phone. She looked at the alarm clock beside the bed and realized she'd overslept again after another bad night.

She groped for the phone and sat up as she brought it to her ear. A heavily accented voice on the other end began telling her the benefits of new carefree siding for her home. "Actually, the siding is just fine on both my houses," she said. "Thank you." Then she hung up before the young man could launch into a new pitch.

"At least I'm up," she said quietly as she slipped her feet into her slippers. Boots poked her head around the corner and greeted her with a quizzical meow.

"Thanks for not waking me with chest compressions this morning," Annie said.

Boots padded into the room and rubbed against Annie's ankles as she shrugged into her robe. "I believe I dreamed about a dog last night," she teased the gray cat. "I hope you're not too jealous."

Boots showed no sign of jealousy as she led the way to the kitchen for their morning tea and crunchies.

Annie and Alice had a date after lunch to search the attic for the tea set and any other toys that might be packed away.

Until then, Annie planned to transfer several flats of pansies into low, round planters fashioned to look like wooden barrels. The flowers would add instant color to several spots in the yard that seemed a bit bare. She slipped into her gardening outfit of cropped jeans and a paint-splattered T-shirt she'd accidentally adorned while repainting the kitchen. The yummy golden vanilla looked great in the kitchen but slightly less attractive on the sleeves and hem of the blue shirt. She pulled her fine blond hair into a loose ponytail and stepped out on the front porch.

The day was gray and the haze had turned to chilly rain. Annie wrapped her arms around herself and realized she'd need a jacket just to stand on the porch for long. She definitely didn't want to try to plant in this weather. At least she didn't have to worry about the pansies drying out. Annie looked out at the gloom and the rain, and shivered as another nudge of déjà vu prodded her.

The rain made her feel anxious and unsettled. Or maybe it was the thought of making the final decision about Stony Point. She certainly didn't want her wishy-washy behavior to last a full year—Gram would have been horrified at Annie putting it off so long, and Wayne would have told her to "make a decision and commit to it." In some way, she felt a bit like she was letting them down, shifting back and forth. She knew it was time to choose.

When she was a kid visiting Gram, Annie had always felt crushingly sad when she'd gone home and left Stony Point behind. She and Alice always concocted the craziest schemes at the end of summer. Though Annie had to admit, Alice was much better at coming up with wild ideas than she was. More than once, Annie had left for Texas without getting to say goodbye to her best friend, because Alice was grounded after some crazy adventure of theirs ended in disaster. It always felt as if they had to cram a whole year into those last weeks each summer.

If she decided to stay in Texas, these would be her last weeks of living at Grey Gables. She should fill the days with fun and friends instead of indecision and worry. Maybe she'd even try a wild idea or two with Alice.

Thinking of Alice brought her back to the attic. She'd planned to wait for Alice before searching for the tea set, but she was too restless to curl up with a book or to work on her crochet. She would just dash up and collect the tea set since she knew where it was, and maybe earmark some of the most likely boxes to check for other toys.

When she reached the top of the attic stairs and looked around, she sighed. She'd already spent hours up here, putting the attic in order. She had to admit that she hadn't gotten rid of much, but at least most of the boxes were sorted and labeled. Or so she'd thought.

As she looked over the crowded attic, there were still so many chests and boxes she hadn't opened. She'd hoped to finish sorting and organizing all the boxes and trunks in the attic before heading to Texas for her grandchildren's birthday party, but every day was so full of things to do that this task kept getting pushed aside.

She slipped through the maze of boxes until she reached the old bird's-eye maple dressing table where she'd left the tea set when they first unearthed it. The small wicker basket with the miniature moss-rose tea set inside still rested right on top. Annie was pleased to see it hadn't begun collecting dust yet. She turned the tarnished latch on the basket and looked at the tiny cups and saucers nestled in the blue gingham lining of the basket. The set would look lovely in a display, set up as if inviting the viewer to join a tea party.

Someday, she planned to give the set to her granddaughter, but with John as Joanna's main playmate right now, Annie suspected the tiny dishes wouldn't last long. Maybe next year. Maybe she should wait until the tea set could be more of a family heirloom than a plaything.

Annie turned and looked over the rest of the attic. Would it be enough to simply send the one item for the library display? She hadn't actually run across any other toys during her searches of the attic, but that didn't mean they weren't there, nestled among all the other mysteries in the unopened past.

Rain drummed on the roof over her head as she leaned on the dressing table. The gloom outside pressed against the attic windows, deepening the shadows inside. Even though Annie had done a lot to clean the attic, it was still a creepy place to spend a rainy morning alone.

Suddenly Annie heard a rustle from the far corner where a dressmaker's mannequin stood. The mannequin was swathed from top to bottom in a white sheet that was now yellowed with age and dust, giving it the impression of a shroud. On top of the headless mannequin, someone had tossed a sorry-looking hat that had been decorated with silk cabbage roses and trailing ribbons that were now wilted and faded.

As she heard another rustle, Annie shuddered. Surely more mice hadn't moved into the house? She'd thought her handyman, Wally Carson, had solved the problem and blocked up their entry points to the house, but she knew there were few creatures more tenacious than mice.

Then, as she peered into the gloom, the hat on top of the mannequin turned slowly as if the wrapped figure were turning to look at her. Annie's hand flew to her chest, and she gasped in the dusty air. Just then, she heard a familiar sneeze.

"Boots," Annie scolded. "You scared me half to death." She slipped through the boxes and spotted the gray cat in the shadows, batting at one of the trailing ribbons on the hat. Annie scooped up the cat and gave her a gentle hug. "Who needs ghosts when I have you?" she asked.

"Annie!"

Annie turned toward the stairs and hurried across the attic, still cradling the purring cat. "Alice?" she called down. "I'm already in the attic. Come on up!"

Alice appeared at the top of the stairs wearing very un-characteristic faded jeans, a long button-down shirt with the sleeves rolled up, and a bandanna covering most of her shoulder-length auburn hair. "You started without me," she said shaking a finger at Annie with a mock pout.

"Not really. I haven't opened anything except the wicker basket with the tea set," Annie said. She lifted the cat slightly in her arms. "I was interrupted by a haunting."

"Oh?" Alice's eyes flashed with curiosity that turned to laughter as Annie told her about Boots playing ghost for her. "Oh, that reminds me of the stormy afternoons we spent up here scaring each other half to death with ghost stories."

Annie shook her head smiling. "And you know, I don't think I remember a single one of them."

"Really? I remember them all. My favorite was the lighthouse ghosts. You must remember that one."

Annie wrinkled her forehead as she thought. "Something about a curse, right?"

"You do remember," Alice said, slipping by Annie to point out the far attic window toward the coastline. "Anyone who dares to touch the lighthouse without invitation on a stormy night will be haunted by the wailing ghosts of the cliffs before dawn."

Annie nodded as she gently put Boots on the floor. "That does sound familiar now. I'm surprised you never tried it."

"What makes you think I never tried it?" Alice asked, grinning.

"You did?" Annie gaped at her friend. "I can't believe it. I was scared to death of the lighthouse keeper. What was his name?"

"Murdoch," Alice said, giving a pretend shudder of fear. "Believe me, he was even scarier on a stormy night. I thought I would die of fright when he came roaring off the porch of the lighthouse keeper's cottage, shining a flashlight in everyone's eyes and ranting like a crazy person. Some of the guys managed to run off, but he caught me and called my folks. Honestly, by then, I was just glad he didn't kill me with an ax. I was grounded for a month, but everyone at school thought I was fearless."

"As I remember, you pretty much were," Alice said, then she turned and gestured across the attic. "We have the tea set. Do you think it's worth poking around for anything else?"

"Sure," Alice said. "It'll be fun. Besides, I don't want to waste my attic-adventuring outfit. Point me at boxes that remain unopened!"

# ~4~

nnie slipped between the neat rows to where the attic still looked a bit jumbled. Cardboard boxes tied with twine were stacked two or three high, and a few old trunks stood behind the stacks of boxes, sometimes with a smaller box or two sitting on their lids. "It's pretty easy to see what parts I haven't reached yet," she said.

"Let's start with a trunk," Alice said. "They always make me think of ocean voyages and foreign lands."

"I don't know that I would count on finding anything that exotic," Annie said, as she lifted a twine-bound box from the top of a small brown trunk. They knelt in front of the trunk as they hauled it open. A puff of dust wafted off the lid, making Annie sneeze.

The trunk had a top tray that held delicate baby clothes wrapped in tissue. Each tiny dress was trimmed in some kind of needlework, bits of crocheted lace on one and delicate embroidery on another. "What beautiful work!" Alice exclaimed, gently lifting a tiny polka-dot dress that featured a row of circus animals marching across a band of smocking.

Annie nodded. "It could be Gram's. She told me she'd tried a lot of different kinds of needlework before she settled on cross-stitch. Maybe she tried most of them while she was pregnant with my mom."

"If she did," Alice said. "She must have been good at everything!"

"That sounds like Gram," Annie responded as she gently folded the dresses back up in the tissue and laid them in the trunk. "I don't know whether to frame them or hope for another granddaughter."

"You might want to give LeeAnn a vote in that," Alice said. "Seems like she has her hands full with the twins. I know the very thought of twins is enough to give me nightmares!"

"I can't imagine how she does it sometimes." Annie lifted out the tray and began sorting through a layer of old books underneath. "But she's very capable. I think she took after Gram in that way." She held up a book. "*The Secret Garden*. This is a beautiful copy. Someone took good care of it. Do you suppose the library would like some old kids' books for the display?"

"Maybe, though Valerie may already be planning to use books from the library in the display. We could set them aside just in case and ask her."

Annie nodded and put the books off to one side. At the bottom of the trunk, she found a long, narrow box and lifted it out. Another book had been wedged between the box and the back of the trunk. It tumbled to the bottom when Annie lifted the box. She reached down between two other boxes and snagged the book by the corner. Then she added it to the pile. The box she'd removed looked almost like a flower box, but the cardboard was thick and stained, and the box was wrapped in loop after loop of twine.

"Wow, that looks like someone was afraid something inside was going to escape," Alice said with a laugh.

"Oh, thanks," Annie said, setting the box down quickly. "That's a creepy image. I don't think I would enjoy finding a chipmunk mummy or some other dead critter inside."

"Aren't we going to open it?" Alice asked, picking the box up and turning it over in her hands. Inside something shifted with a rustle and soft thud. "You don't want to pass up a mystery do you?"

"I don't know. Do you think it might be something dead? I've had a lot of mysteries in the past months. I thought I might go with a nice quiet week or two."

"Wimp," Alice said, grinning. She shifted the box again. "I don't suppose you brought scissors or a knife up here with you?"

Annie shook her head. "We could take it downstairs."

"No. If it turns out to be boring, I want to look some more." She brought it closer to her face to look over the knot on the underside of the box and began picking at it.

While she wrestled with the knot, Annie put the tray back in the trunk and closed the lid. Then she gathered up the books and carried them over to the maple dressing table so she would know where to find them if the librarian showed an interest.

"Got it!" Alice crowed after a few minutes. She unwrapped the string and held out the box. "Do you want to do the honors?"

"After your remark about something being trapped in there?" Annie said, holding up a hand. "Be my guest."

Alice pulled the lid from the box. Inside, a slightly tattered rag doll lay in a nest of newspaper. "Oh, my," Alice said. "Who would wrap a doll in newspaper? The ink has made her dress even grubbier."

"A child might," Annie said as she walked over to look closely at the doll. It had thick black wool hair and a sweet embroidered face with black button eyes. The muslin face was stained, showing where the black dye of the wool had run slightly onto the fabric. "Looks like the doll got wet. You know, there's something familiar about this doll."

"Maybe it belonged to your mother," Alice suggested.

Annie stared into the doll's scuffed button eyes and shook her head. "My mother wasn't a doll girl. Gram used to talk about that like it was some kind of affliction. I think she would have loved to fill my mother's room with dolls." Anne bit her lower lip gently between her teeth as she looked over the doll's old dress. "This is handmade. Why would someone go to that kind of trouble for a girl who didn't like dolls?"

Alice shrugged. "Maybe it was made by a relative. Sometimes they can be kind of clueless. Do you remember the honeybee pinafore Nana Muriel made for me when I was twelve?"

"Oh, yeah, I remember," Annie said, laughing at the memory. "Your mother insisted you wear it for the Fourth of July picnic to show respect for you grandmother."

"I would have worn it," Alice said. "If I hadn't fallen down the front-porch steps right as we were getting ready to leave, and I got that terrible grass stain on it."

Annie burst out laughing. "As I remember, you fell down and then rolled yourself halfway across the front lawn before your Mom came outside."

"What can I say?" Alice said primly. "I was a clumsy child. Honeybees, ugh!" She shuddered, and then burst into giggles. The two women laughed until they were gasping.

Holding the doll, Annie stood up. "Well, I'll consider putting it in the display, but I don't think it was my mother's. It's not like the honeybee pinafore. Clearly this doll saw a lot of loving and cuddling."

"Hey, I cuddled the pinafore in my own way," Alice said as she walked back to the dressing table and picked up the box with the little tea set. "This makes two toys; that's probably enough."

Annie nodded absently as she followed Alice down the attic stairs. She carried the doll to the table in the kitchen and propped it up beside the tea-set basket. "Would you like some tea?"

"Sounds like the perfect gloomy-cold-day drink," Alice said. "I'm sorry I didn't bring a snack to go with it. I have another new muffin recipe that uses blueberries, lemon and almonds."

Annie carried a tin of shortbread to the table to go with their dark English tea, perfect for chasing away the cobwebs that seemed to be in her head lately. "You don't always have to feed me," she said with a smile. "But if you *want* to bring over some muffins sometime, I won't resist."

"I knew you'd like the sound of those. So what do you think of our new mystery lady?" Alice gestured toward the doll. The dull light coming through the kitchen windows cast a shadow over the doll's face, making her embroidered smile seem melancholy. "Maybe it was Betsy's?"

"I don't think it looks old enough to have been Gram's. It's nicely made though. Someone put a lot of time into it."

"Except this part," Alice pointed to a ragged bit of stitching on the doll's apron. "Is that a bird? It looks like it was done by a little kid."

Annie lifted the doll and looked at the apron. Faded blue stitching on the apron *did* look like a bird if you added a lot of imagination. "I think it is a bird. A bird with a pointed head."

Alice laughed. "Poor bird. So we don't think it belonged to Betsy or your mother. You know what *that* means."

Annie looked up at her friend's wide grin and shook her head, trying to ward off the inevitable. "A mystery!" Alice announced.

# ~5~

Annie didn't have time to scold Alice for the "m" word, because the women heard a knock at the front door. "I'm so popular lately," Annie said as they walked to the door.

They found Wally Carson grinning sheepishly at them through the screen door. Annie knew he was scrambling to catch up on a number of handyman jobs that had piled up after he'd broken his arm the previous summer. She hadn't really had him back to Grey Gables since they'd dealt with the mice and all the chewed-up wiring. She loved the careful work Wally did, but she knew Wally's handyman skills were much sought after, and Annie didn't want to be greedy. Plus, if she were totally honest, she needed a little break from hammering and painting. Wally had been a lifesaver when she'd arrived in Stony Point and seen how much Gram's house had fallen into disrepair, but he'd done so much that she thought they could both take a bit of a break.

The old house felt more like a home again and less like a project because of all the things Wally had done for her. Still, she wondered if it might be wise to make up a list of possible spring and summer projects so she wouldn't end up last in line for the busy handyman's time. "Did you spot something I need to have mended?" Annie asked with a smile.

"In a way," Wally said, backing away from the door and

gesturing toward a spot on the porch they couldn't see. Annie slipped through the door and saw a wicker chair with a lovely striped cushion that matched the other chairs on the porch. "I didn't get a chance to work on that chair you bought at the charity auction last year before I broke my arm, and then I've been tied up with that cabinet installation job and trying to catch up on things people needed. Anyway, your chair has been sitting in my workshop, and I totally forgot about it." He grinned again. "Sorry about that. It's good as new now, though. Just in time for the weather to warm up so you can enjoy it. And Peggy made the cushion to help make up for how long you had to wait."

"That does help *cushion* the blow," Alice said.

Annie and Wally both groaned together at Alice's horrible pun, making her friend laugh. "Sorry, sorry. I couldn't help myself!"

"Well, the chair looks lovely," Annie said as she stepped closer to look at it. She walked in a full circle around it and couldn't spot any of Wally's mending. It looked perfect. "I thought I'd made a huge mistake when I accidentally bought a three-legged chair, but you did a wonderful job. You're amazing."

"I told you that you got a great bargain," Alice said.

"As I remember, you told me that I'd gotten caught up in auction fever." Annie turned back to Wally. "You've probably saved me from a lot of teasing with your gorgeous work."

Wally blushed a bit at the praise. "I wanted to do a good job for you. You've done a lot for us since you came to town."

"And you've done a lot for Grey Gables," Annie said, gesturing at the house. "You've really brought this old

Victorian back to the way Gram would have wanted it."

Wally had worked steadily on the house ever since Annie arrived back in Stony Point, right up until he'd fallen out of a tree and broken his arm. Annie's few attempts at home repairs during his healing made her all the more grateful to have such an excellent handyman. And she liked knowing she was helping out his family. She loved Peggy and their adorable princess-loving daughter.

"It's been good to have the work."

As Annie slipped inside to get her wallet, Alice said a quick goodbye since she needed to prepare for one of her jewelry parties. "Don't take that doll to the library until everyone sees it at the Hook and Needle meeting," she called out to Annie. "Stella might recognize it. Or someone else."

"You just want to turn it into a mystery," Annie scolded as she carried the check back out to Wally.

"We all love a good mystery," Alice agreed with no sign of remorse. She waved at both of them and trotted down the porch steps.

Having Alice around is like reconnecting with a lost sister, Annie thought with a smile, as she watched her friend hurry out to her flashy Mustang convertible. Somehow Alice always looked totally at home in that car, with the wind blowing her auburn hair. Annie couldn't imagine driving something so attention-getting.

"Thank you," Wally said as she handed him the check for the work on the chair. "Let me know if there's anything else I can do for you."

"I will," Annie agreed. "Are you still putting in some time on Todd Butler's lobster boat?"

"On and off when they need the help," Wally said as he pushed back a heavy lock of dark hair. "He's got a sweet boat."

When Wally left, Annie walked back into the house; she thought about the talented handyman's longing to be a fisherman. She wished she could just give Wally the money for a boat of his own. Even though Wayne had provided well for her, she was far from wealthy. Still, she knew how he longed to be out on the water. He came from a fishing family that had fallen on hard times. She wondered how Peggy would feel about Wally going out to sea with his own boat. Lobster fishing wasn't exactly like an episode of *Deadliest Catch*, but anytime you're out on the water, you run risks.

"I'd make a terrible fairy godmother," she decided. She'd constantly be second-guessing whether she'd made someone's life better or just more complicated. As she walked into the kitchen to grab a second cup of coffee, she immediately noticed the rag doll was missing from the table.

"Oh no!" Annie froze. She'd had people creep into her house more than once since arriving at Grey Gables, and she'd even had her car broken into. It was one reason she was less than excited about the idea of a new mystery. And now the doll was missing. Did she have someone new creeping around the house? Usually the stalkers waited until she'd *told* someone about the mystery!

She looked under the table, but the doll hadn't simply fallen onto the floor. Goose bumps crept up her arms as she wondered if the thief could still be in the house with her. She walked quietly across the kitchen and pulled open one of the deep drawers and looked inside for a possible weapon.

A solid rolling pin looked like the best choice, so she slipped it quietly out and silently pushed the drawer closed.

Then as she turned back into the room, she spotted a flash of movement near the floor out of the corner of her eye. Boot's tail twitched from where the cat had crept between the end of the counter and the wall. Had the burglar frightened the cat? That didn't seem likely since Boots had turned into a fuzzy ball of claws and temper when she'd had a thief in the house once before. "Boots," she whispered. "Boots!"

The chubby cat actually growled from her tight confines, and Annie suddenly felt a bit suspicious. What if this theft was an inside job? She opened the drawer again, this time fishing out the heavy flashlight Gram always kept there, and returning the rolling pin with a shake of her head. All this mystery talk was making her jumpy again.

Annie flashed the light into the narrow gap between the cabinets and wall. She caught sight of dark yarn hair and a pale muslin face, then the flash reflected off the cat's eyes as Boots huddled over her prize. "Boots!" she said. "You come out of there with that doll."

Boots responded with another growl. What had gotten into that cat? No amount of coaxing could get Boots to come out of her corner and tugging lightly on her tail had resulted in such a fierce growl that Annie decided not to repeat the gesture.

She finally had to resort to opening a can of tuna to draw the cat out of the tight space. Then, while Boots gobbled down tuna, Annie reached in and retrieved the doll. She looked it over carefully. Boots didn't appear to have clawed it anywhere, though some of the yarn hair was suspiciously damp.

"This isn't a kitten; it doesn't need grooming," Annie told the cat. Boots looked up and licked her lips smugly. "You are incorrigible. I'd better find a safer place for this doll."

Annie tucked the doll under the yarn in her project bag. Since she had gotten into the habit of keeping that bag out of reach from curious paws already, she'd be taking care of two problems at once when she hung the bag high on a peg.

The rain settled in for a long, gray stay, and Annie found it to be perfect crocheting weather. She finished Joanna's sweater during the three-day New England monsoon; she found that she slept surprisingly well. She'd expected more visits from her recurring nightmare with the sound of rain pounding on the roof, but perhaps it had passed.

On the third day, when the sun struggled to peek through the thinning clouds, Annie was glad for the chance to get outside again. She looked over the sodden flower beds, knowing it was a great time for weeding since the ground would be soft. She reached down and pulled up one glob of dandelion and mud. She laid it on one of the rocks that bordered the bed and brushed off her hands. "Maybe later."

After a quick wash of her hands, she grabbed her project bag and the tea set, and headed for town instead. The weeds could wait.

The rain-darkened streets were lightening up as they dried in the few rays of sun struggling to peek out of the clouds. By the time she parked in front of A Stitch in Time, the sun had won the battle. Annie climbed out of the car and looked around, enjoying the smell and look of the rain-washed town.

Then she looked down one street, and her breath caught

in her throat. A rainbow. Annie's mother had loved rainbows, and for a moment, Annie could hear her voice in her mind. "Every rainbow is a promise, Annie," she'd said. "They remind us that God has a plan for this world."

"God has a plan," Annie echoed softly. Sometimes it was hard to remember that a bigger plan was at work. She was glad for reminders. That was something Gram was good at too, reminding Annie of the things that were real and true.

Annie thought of the day she'd called Gram, not long after Wayne's death. Annie had been so lost without him. "Why is life about loss, Gram?" she'd asked, sobbing. "Mom, Dad, Wayne—loss after loss."

"Annie," Gram had said in her gentle voice, "life isn't about loss. It's about gain. Your mom, your dad, and Wayne. You had each of those amazing people in your life. They loved you, changed you and helped you become the woman you are. How blessed you've been."

And with that, Annie had started, just started, on the road to healing. She still had a long way to go. "But I'm getting there," she murmured.

She was pulled from her thoughts by a gentle bump.

"Oh, excuse me!"

Annie turned as a frazzled mom smiled at her apologetically. The woman was weighed down with packages and struggled to keep the hand of a squirming little boy who howled when she wouldn't let go.

"Do let me help," Annie said, taking some of the packages from the woman's arms and smiling at the child. He stopped pulling on his mom as he stared at Annie. *Nothing like a stranger to distract a little one from fussing*, Annie thought.

The woman thanked her several times as Annie followed her to a dark green SUV parked in front of Malone's Hardware. "There's just so much involved in opening up the house for the year," the woman said wearily. "I think I forget during the fall and winter. Otherwise, I wouldn't be so eager to start this up again each spring."

Annie nodded as she piled the packages into the car while the woman hefted her little boy into his car seat. The child peeked around his mother and offered Annie a small solemn wave. Annie waved back. "Have a good summer," she said.

"That would be nice," the woman agreed as she closed the backseat door and pulled open her own. "Maybe I'll see you around Stony Point. Thanks again for helping."

As Annie backed away from the SUV, she wondered if the young woman would see her around. Maybe she should begin planning how to close up Grey Gables, just in case she didn't come back from Texas. The thought caused a pang to hit her stomach like a hammer. How could she leave here? Wasn't this home now?

# ~6~

nnie was surprised to find Alice already at A Stitch in Time when she got there.

"Fancy meeting you here, neighbor," Annie said, putting on her broadest Texas accent.

Alice held up a tiny pair of cloth shoes. "I brought these for the library doll. If they fit, I thought we could embroider something on them to match the theme. Once we decide on the theme."

"Not to be nosy," Mary Beth said, the sparkle in her eyes showing just how comfortable she was with being totally nosy, "but why do you just happen to have a pair of preemie baby shoes?"

"I have a whole box of baby shoes," Alice said with a sigh. "I bought them at an outlet store in Portland two years ago last fall. I planned to decorate them with embroidery and trims over the winter, and then sell them to tourists. It's one of my money-making schemes that never really came to anything. I didn't have as much lonely work time this winter as I usually have." She grinned in Annie's direction. "Too many mysteries kept me busy."

"I think all the Princessa jewelry and Divine Décor parties deserve far more of the credit," Annie insisted. "I don't think I've been inside a house in Stony Point where I don't spot bits of Divine Décor, and that includes Grey Gables."

"Gotta make a living," Alice said.

"With everything you do," Mary Beth said, "I wouldn't be surprised if you said you didn't have time to breathe. Still, if you ever do embroider the shoes, let me know and we'll put some in the shop. It does sound like something tourists would like."

Annie smiled at her two friends. They were both incredibly business-minded, and Annie admired them for that. Wayne had been the businessman in their family, and now LeeAnn tended to take after him. Annie was good with numbers and perfectly happy to handle the books at their car dealership, but she was more prone to going with the flow than coming up with new ways to blaze a trail.

"Did you need more yarn for your granddaughter's sweater?" Mary Beth asked, shaking Annie out of her wandering thoughts. "Or are you in need of something new? I have some yummy pastel cotton yarn that I hoped to tempt you with. You'd look gorgeous in the sea greens."

"I actually finished Joanna's sweater," Annie said. "The rain was wonderful for my work ethic. I wanted to show the sweater to Kate. Is she coming in today?"

Mary Beth nodded. "She's grabbing lunch for both of us from The Cup & Saucer. They're so busy over there today with everyone rushing in after the rain that Peggy couldn't break away to bring us something."

"Speaking of bringing us something," Alice said, "did you bring in the new mystery from the attic?"

"Only because I'm planning to take it over to the library with the tea set," Annie said. "But the only mystery here is why Boots decided she wanted to claim the doll for herself."

At Mary Beth's quizzical look, Annie pulled the doll from her bag and set it on the table while she told them about the way Boots kidnapped it from the table. She sheepishly admitted she'd been worried she had a burglar.

"You do," Alice said laughing. "A cat burglar."

The women moaned at Alice's pun, and then Mary Beth added, "I don't blame you for being jumpy. You've had more than your share of scary things since you got here, and they've all been connected to the attic."

"I'm just glad I didn't call the police when the doll disappeared," Annie said. "Can you imagine how embarrassing that would have been? I've already seen more than one of the young policemen around here look at me like I was imagining things when I've called before."

"And you were always proven totally right," Alice said, firmly defending her friend. "And you can always call me, you know."

"Well, this time I didn't really need to call anyone, and I'm glad. It's about time the attic produced something not totally scary," Annie said, gently smoothing the doll's dress. "She's just a nice simple rag doll."

"Was she yours?" Mary Beth asked.

Annie shook her head. "I've never seen her before, but she's nicely made. I don't know who she belonged to. Clearly someone loved her a lot. I'd love to get her back to the owner, but I don't have much to go on."

Mary Beth felt the fabrics. "These are fairly modern bits in the clothes, so she couldn't have been from Betsy's childhood. Maybe she belonged to your mom."

"Annie already ruled her out," Alice said. "Not a dolly girl."

"I could see someone making it for her," Annie said. "Every girl ends up with a doll at some time or other. But this one was clearly loved, and Gram always said Mom never liked dolls. She was more of a tomboy apparently."

The bell over the door jangled as Annie spoke, and they turned to see Kate with Ian trailing after her, carrying a small pile of foam takeout boxes. "Look who followed me home," Kate said with a laugh. "He even insisted on carrying my heavy burdens."

"Hey, they can't be too heavy. I don't eat that much," Mary Beth said, smoothing her long cotton sweater over her slightly padded figure.

"I'm sure you eat like a bird," Ian said, setting the containers on the counter.

"Of course, the Discovery Channel says most birds eat half their weight in food every day," Alice put in with a grin.

Ian held up his hands in mock surrender. "I give up," he said. "I do not intend to get involved in any discussion that includes women, food and weight. It's time for me to escape while I'm still alive, but I would like to take Annie with me. Smelling those lunch containers made me hungry. Would you join me for lunch, Annie?"

"I'd like that," Annie said, "but I wanted to show my granddaughter's sweater to Kate first. I finished it!"

Kate admired the bright beads, bits of embroidery, and the lacy look of the sweater's edging. "I think she'll like this," she said. "It's very girlie. What are you planning to do for John?"

"I really don't know," Annie said, thinking of her rambunctious grandson. "I don't think he would be excited about a sweater. He's always nice about my crocheted gifts, but I'd really like to give him something that wows him this time. And it's hard to wow a little boy with yarn."

"I can see how that would be a problem," Kate agreed. Then she picked up the rag doll. "Whose is this?"

"I found it in the attic," Annie said. "I don't know who it belonged to. I'm going to put it in the old toy display at the library."

Kate gently straightened the doll's long yarn hair. "It was clearly well-loved. There's something sad about an old doll. Imagine all the secrets she's heard, and the scary things she kept at bay. Now she's all alone—just a reminder of growing up and away from the simple things."

"Spoken like the mother of a teenager," Mary Beth said.

Kate nodded. "It was tough seeing Vanessa outgrow dolls. She never had a rag doll like this, though. It's a real beauty. There's so much personality in a homemade doll. What's this on the apron?"

"Some kind of bird," Alice said. "Whoever owned it must have been trying her hand at needlework."

Kate nodded. "Who knows? Maybe she grew up to love embroidery and comes in here all the time? You know who you should ask about it? Stella. She was here when she was young. She might remember it."

"I don't think it goes back to Stella's childhood," Annie said, "but I still might ask her. I'll hang onto it until the next Hook and Needle session. But then it's off to the library. I really don't need another mystery with everything else in my life right now."

"We don't always get to pick our mysteries," Alice said,

crossing her arms and leaning against the counter. "Sometimes they pick us."

"And on that ominous note," Ian cut in, "can we solve the mystery of whether the mayor is going to starve in the presence of the most lovely ladies of Stony Point?"

"Only Ian could mix a complaint and a compliment in one smooth package," Mary Beth said, laughing. "You should go let the man eat, Annie. If he collapses, I'm not certain we could pick him up."

"That's OK," Alice said. "You could throw an afghan over his body and use him for additional seating.

"We'd better go before they redesign me as a lamp," Ian said, guiding Annie toward the door with a hand at her back.

As Annie and Ian headed toward the door, Annie glanced back to see all three women grinning at her. She knew that the one thing they loved more than a mystery was a romance. She smiled in affection and shook her head gently.

"What?" Ian asked, glancing at her as he held the door.

"Just thinking about what good friends I've found here in Stony Point," she said.

"Enough good friends to make you finally decide to stay?" he asked, quizzically raising a single dark eyebrow.

"Enough to make staying very tempting," she answered as she looked back down the street for a glimpse of the rainbow she'd seen earlier. But it was gone. Then she turned and glanced up at Ian's familiar profile. Ian had high cheekbones and a strong jaw. Wayne's face was square and boyish. Wayne had always kept the sturdy build that reflected his years playing college football, while Ian was slender but broad-shouldered.

Though he looked totally different, Ian's warmth and charm often brought up memories of Wayne so sharply they took Annie's breath away. No matter what the ladies of the Hook and Needle Club hoped, Annie definitely wasn't ready for romance yet.

Ian looked down. "We do try to be tempting."

Annie blinked, taking a moment to relate his comment to her last remark. Her woolgathering seemed to be getting worse. *Pretty soon I'll be able to make a sweater from all the wool I've gathered*, she thought.

Ian pulled open the door to the diner and stepped aside so Annie could enter. Peggy caught sight of them and waved brightly, her short, dark hair bouncing with her excitement. She pointed toward an empty table near the front windows.

Ian gallantly held Annie's chair as she sat, and then took a seat opposite her as Peggy rushed over with a coffeepot in hand. "Do you need menus?" she asked as she turned over the coffee mugs on the table and poured the rich-smelling coffee. "We're having a chilly day, Mr. Mayor. Is it officially a soup day? I'm never sure during the spring."

"I've become horribly predictable," Ian said in protest.

"Not predictable," Peggy insisted, "comfortable."

He shook his head, a smile pulling at the corners of his mouth. "That sounds even worse. Now I feel like a chair."

"I give up," Peggy said. She straightened up and asked very formally. "Good day, sir. What would you like?"

After a pause, Ian asked, "What kind of soup do you have?"

Annie and Peggy burst out laughing together. Then Peggy named off the soups, and Ian chose the corn chowder.

Annie asked for the same, and Peggy rushed away.

"Well, I'm predictable, but you're always full of surprises," Ian said, his chocolate brown eyes warm as he looked across the table. "What are you doing these days? How are the repairs going on Grey Gables?"

"I'm actually almost running out of things to do. Not that you ever run out of home repairs, but the house feels safe and looks the way Gram would approve of again. So, I haven't really been doing anything terribly interesting," Annie said. "I finished a birthday present for Joanna, as you saw. I'm totally stuck on what to give John. You were once a little boy. Maybe you can help. I want to give him something really personal, but I don't think there's anything I can crochet that would wow him."

"Maybe you could buy him a toolbox," Ian said. "I think I was about that age when my father gave me a toolbox."

"I suspect my daughter would not be pleased if I armed John with a saw and a hammer," Annie said. "I can imagine the carnage. She'd have three-legged tables and boards nailed to every wall."

"If you ever lure LeeAnn here with the children, I could get Todd to give him a ride on the boat," Ian said. "Sometimes Todd takes members of our family out on a private whale watch. You should come; it's amazing to see the whales. You really never get tired of it. They're breathtaking every single time."

"I'd like that," Annie said, "and John would love it. He's been crazy about boats since he saw his first pirate movie."

Peggy arrived with two thick crocks of chowder and small bags of oyster crackers on the side. As she put the crocks on the table, she cut her eyes toward Annie. "You weren't mad about how long it took Wally to fix your chair, were you?"

"No, of course not," Annie shook her head. "I had nearly forgotten I bought it. He did a wonderful job with the repair. It looks like it was never broken. And the cushion you made matched perfectly."

"I'm glad." Peggy's face lit up. "Wally does do wonderful work, doesn't he? I told him you wouldn't be upset about the wait. It took him almost that long to make that bird palace that Gwendolyn Palmer designed last year. You should see that thing. It's huge, but definitely pretty. Gwen really has a unique sense of style."

Annie stared at her for a moment, an idea dawning. "Do you think Wally could make a boat?"

Peggy laughed. "If he could, he sure would have by now. I think that's a little bigger project than he could put together out in our little shed."

"No, I'm sorry. I meant a toy boat. I suddenly thought *that* would be the perfect present for my grandson. He loves boats, and it would be something homemade. Do you think Wally could do something like that? I don't know if it would be harder than a bird palace. I think Gwen said she drew sketches for that birdhouse, but I really don't have many ideas about what a boat should look like."

"I'm sure he could do it." Peggy's face nearly glowed with pride. "And he'd like it even better if all the details were up to him. Do you want me to ask him?"

"Please do," Annie said, "and tell him I'd expect to pay well for it. I want something special for John."

"I will," Peggy practically floated away, clearly happy at the thought of a new, paying project for Wally. Peggy and Wally both worked hard, but it could be a struggle, especially with Wally having missed some lucrative handyman time last summer with his broken arm. Annie knew that sometimes a few months of lost income took far longer to make up. At least Ian's brother had found him some work aboard the lobster boat while his arm was healing.

"Another good deed by Annie Dawson," Ian said as they gazed after the young waitress as she wove in and out of the tables with new energy.

"Wally will be the one doing the good deed if he can make that boat," Annie said as she spooned up some chowder. "I was really stumped for a gift, and that would be perfect."

Ian saluted her with his coffee cup. "I still say you spread good cheer wherever you go."

"That wasn't always the case around here."

He set the cup down and leaned forward to look at her intently. "It has always been the case with me."

Startled by the suddenly intimate tone, Annie stared at Ian's handsome face for a moment, not knowing what to say. Then his serious expression broke into a smile, and he turned his attention to his soup. "This looks delicious."

Annie nodded, happy for the chance to look back at her own soup. Surely Ian was just as happy with their friendship as she was, wasn't he? He was a handsome man, and she certainly enjoyed the attention, but she wasn't ready for more than friendship. Was he looking for more than that?

Annie felt slightly off balance through the rest of lunch and was almost relieved when Ian excused himself to get back to City Hall. She sipped her coffee silently for a while; then she sighed and gave herself a mental shake. She'd been doing too much woolgathering lately, and it was time to stop before she drowned under a mountain of woolly daydreams.

*I need to be more like Gram,* she thought as she strode toward the diner door. *If I were, I wouldn't have spent the summer flipping back and forth over what I want to do.*

In her rush, Annie pushed open the door just as someone pulled from the other side, and she nearly fell into the arms of a tall, bearded man who rocked back awkwardly.

"Oh, I'm so sorry," Annie said as she leaped back from the stranger.

The man caught his balance with the help of a cane and smiled. He had a heavily weathered face, and Annie wondered if he was a local fisherman. He certainly didn't look familiar as he nodded to her slightly. "No apology necessary. I never complain about lovely ladies falling on me."

Annie blushed furiously as she stammered a bit and slipped around the stranger. What was it with the men of Stony Point lately? She was so flustered that she headed back to Grey Gables without picking up the rag doll from A Stitch in Time.

# 7

The young, dark-haired girl hurries down the sodden gravel road. Rain runs down her nose and chin, and her wet dress clings to her legs as if trying to trip her. She can hear shouts behind her as her sister and her friend call her name, begging her to stop. She isn't going back, and she isn't waiting on them. This was a stupid idea. What does it matter if it was her idea? They should have gone home when it got scary. Now they are going to be in big trouble.

She grips her doll close to her chest, hoping the soaking rain doesn't ruin her. Gravel slips and slides under her new saddle shoes. Her mother is going to be so mad. They won't be able to hide that they've been out in the rain, not when they're sopping wet and muddy. She sneezes. Her nose and throat are starting to feel raw.

"Jo ought to get in trouble," she mutters. "I hope she does." She stomps her feet, spraying herself with more muddy water from the road. Suddenly, the night lights up brightly around her in a flash of lightning. She sees she's been walking on a diagonal instead of straight down the road. Now she's too close to the cliff edge. The night is black as pitch in the rain. She tries to shift direction, move more to the middle of the narrow road. Her sudden change in direction throws her off balance, and she falls forward, slamming into the ground with enough force to knock the rag doll out of her hands.

*She scrambles forward on her hands and knees, feeling for the doll in the dark. She can't lose the rag doll. It was the last present she ever got from her grandmother. The sharp-edged gravel tears at her knees and mud clings to her skin as she gropes for the doll. Panic wells up in her as she gropes far forward and her hand falls on nothing ...*

Fear of falling jerked Annie awake. She reached quickly for the spiral-bound notebook and pen she'd laid on the bedside table and began writing down as many details as she could remember. Already the sharpness of the images were beginning to fade. She needed to hold on to as much as she could. Annie was certain this dream was important. It must be trying to tell her something, or she wouldn't be having it again and again.

As she finished, she felt the soft thump of Boots landing on the bed. The cat held a bit of paper in her mouth. "What have you gotten into this time?" Annie asked her, reaching out to rub the cat's head and pull the paper from her mouth. The yellowed slip of paper was marred by stains where the ink from the handwriting had run.

The note was written in a child's large, careful printing and said, "Best Friends, Best Fun, Wild Jays Forever!"

"Another clue," Annie said softly. "Now where did you get this?"

Boots just jumped back off the bed with a demanding meow. It was breakfast time and the royal cat expected to be fed.

Later that morning, Annie wandered outside. She told herself she was planning some new plantings for the spring, but her mind wandered back to the dream and the doll and note time after time. She slowly drifted to the edge of the front yard and gazed off toward the lighthouse. She knew now her dream took place on the lighthouse road.

"Oh, there you are!"

Annie turned to see Alice striding across the yard. Her friend wore neatly pressed jeans and a printed blouse in shades of blue and green that set off her auburn hair particularly well. "I walked through the house looking for you," Alice said, "and here you are. You must not have heard me pull up!"

"I had another nightmare," Annie replied, running her fingers through her gray-blonde hair absently. "This time I wrote down some parts of it to help me remember. There were children and Butler's Lighthouse." Annie pointed at the lighthouse on the end of the peninsula. "It was pouring rain, and one of the children was clutching the rag doll. The one we found."

"Sounds like your imagination is gluing together things from the last few days," Alice said and began ticking things off on her fingers as she spoke. "First, we talked about the lighthouse in the attic the other day, remember? How scary it was, and how kids went out in storms to prove they were brave? And then we've had so much rain lately, that's probably why you dreamed about the lighthouse and the rain. The doll came along for the ride because you've wondered who might have owned her."

Annie looked at her friend doubtfully. What she said made sense, but still Annie was sure it was more than that. "Boots brought me this," she said as she handed the scrap of paper to Alice. "I think it must have been tucked into the doll's clothes, and Boots has been playing with it ever since she tried to steal the doll."

Alice smiled at the paper. "Well, that explains that juvenile embroidery. It's probably supposed to be a blue jay."

Annie nodded. "It doesn't explain whose doll it was though."

"I have an idea," Alice said. "Why don't we take a walk to the lighthouse? Since your dream takes place there, maybe it'll stir up some more memories of it. And it's a beautiful day for a walk."

Since Alice's idea of a great walk tended to involve shopping at the end, Annie was a little surprised by the suggestion of a climb up the steep gravel road to the lighthouse. The fact that Alice was wearing socks and bright white sneakers instead of her usual dressy shoes made Annie doubly suspicious. Alice had definitely come over with a walk in mind. Still, it was a lovely day, and Annie had spent too much time brooding lately. "OK, that sounds like fun."

The narrow gravel road that led to Butler's Lighthouse began on the other side of Ocean Drive. It was marked by two rock pillars on either side of a gravel road with a loose chain strung between them after dark. For now, the rusty chain was piled on top of one of the short rock pillars. The pillar also held a small white sign. "Butler's Lighthouse closes at sunset. Absolutely no admittance after dark."

Annie gestured toward the sign. "At least someone is trying to get kids to stop sneaking up there."

Alice laughed sarcastically and rolled her eyes. "Sure!

I know that totally would have made me change my ways when I was a teenager."

The women started up the gravel road. It was a challenging walk and Annie was glad for the cooling breeze as the exertion of the steady uphill grade warmed her. The spring sunshine felt hot on her head and neck, and Annie hoped she didn't get burned because of Alice's mysterious need for a walk.

The wind churned the water to thick, white foam where it struck the half-hidden rocks that made this stretch so dangerous to boats. Huge terns soared and dipped over the water. With her back to Grey Gables, this truly looked like a beautiful, wild place. It was easy to imagine they were stepping into another time.

To their left, a narrow stand of trees separated the lighthouse access road from the steady slope to the beach on the other side. The trees had a stunted look, their limbs twisted by the steady wind off the water. Annie shivered as she imagined how the trees would look after dark. To the right, the gravel road was bordered by a rocky cliff that plummeted to the harbor waters. It was no wonder Gram forbade her to challenge the lighthouse legend.

Finally, they reached the highest point on the peninsula where Butler's Lighthouse watched over the water beyond. The area around the lighthouse was rocky, but Annie could see someone had been working to create raised flower beds filled with bright pansies and azaleas full of buds. She suspected the hand of the Historical Society, as they looked after the property now.

More surprising than the flower beds was the man who

turned to smile at them as they approached. It was the bearded man from The Cup & Saucer. He held a camera and another hung from a strap around his neck. His cane was hooked into the camera strap around his neck to free his hands for taking pictures.

"Hi, Jim!" Alice sang out; her stride had grown positively bouncy.

"Good morning, Alice," the man said. His voice had an attractive gravelly depth to it. He smiled, and his face settled into deep laugh lines around his light eyes. He turned the warm smile on Annie. "And good morning to you too."

"Jim Parker, this is my friend and neighbor, Annie Dawson. She lives next door to me, just down there at the base of the hill on Ocean Drive," Alice said. Annie smiled at her friend's meticulous directions to her house. Annie managed to replace the smile with an interested look just as Alice turned to her. "Jim is working on a book about New England lighthouses. Photos and stories."

"Pleased to meet you, Miz Dawson," Jim said, nodding. A lock of silver hair fell over his eyes. "It's nice to know your name after bumping into you yesterday."

Annie felt heat flush her face, but thankfully he teased her no more about it. "When did you meet Mr. Parker?" Annie asked her friend, suspecting she now understood Alice's special care over her wardrobe today.

"Yesterday at The Cup & Saucer," Alice said. "I was looking for you since you never came back to A Stitch in Time, and I met Jim instead. He told me about his work on this lighthouse project. It's fascinating."

"Alice is being kind about my work," Jim said, "but I do

love these old lighthouses. Not many of them are in actual service anymore. I worry that eventually young people will decide they're too much trouble to keep, so I want to make a record of their history and their legends. I have to admit, taking pictures has been the easy part."

"Oh?" Alice said. "I would think there would be lots of stories with old lighthouses."

"The stories are there," Jim said, shoving the camera in his hand into a case on his hip, "but I've found New England folks aren't overly eager to share them with a stranger. Don't get me wrong. Everyone's been real friendly, just not open to prying questions."

"I know how that is," Annie said, thinking back to her chilly reception from some folks in Stony Point when she'd first arrived. "Have you tried the Historical Society? They look after this property, I think."

"Yup," he said. "I talked to Liz Booth. She let me read clippings and such since she said they were part of the 'historical record.' But she wasn't interested in talking about the legend at all."

"You mean the legend about the curse?" Alice asked, surprise clear in her voice. "That's just silly kid stuff."

"Maybe," Jim said. "I've learned to keep an open mind. I've seen some pretty weird stuff in some of these old lighthouses. Things I couldn't explain. Plus, according to the 'historical record' there have been several deaths of young people connected with this lighthouse and the cliffs around it. One young man was murdered on these cliffs a good many years ago. You ladies were probably kids then."

"He wasn't killed by a curse," Annie said with a shudder since she knew exactly what had killed the dark-eyed young man. That was a story she wasn't likely to forget. "He was killed by a living, breathing person."

Jim shrugged. "Before that, a little girl died on the cliffs too, but I found even less on that story than on the boy."

"A little girl?" Annie said, her voice high. "When? Was she alone?"

"I haven't been able to track down any details at all yet," he said, "but I'm looking. Why? Can you ladies tell me more about this lighthouse curse?"

"I can tell you what I know," Alice said, "but we should sit and get comfortable." She gestured toward the stone benches near the flower beds, another addition from the Historical Society. Jim slipped his cane from the camera strap and used it to limp heavily to the bench. Alice quickly settled beside him, and Annie perched on the edge of a large rock nearby, smiling at how quickly her friend had snagged the seat next to the handsome photographer.

"Long ago," Alice said in her best creepy voice, "Hyrum Matthews took up the job of lighthouse keeper. Old Hyrum hated kids, and kids hated him. Wild boys threw rotten fruit when Hyrum stormed into town for supplies. And groups of kids prowled around the lighthouse keeper's cottage, laughing and scratching at the windows to scare the old man."

"I can see how that could turn you against kids," Jim said, dryly.

"Hush!" Alice said, giving his shoulder a playful push. "You'll break the mood. Anyway, old Hyrum hated those kids, and one night he chased after a bunch of wild boys, waving his lantern and yelling. It was a stormy night ... "

"And dark," Annie inserted, fighting down a giggle at Alice's dramatic retelling of the legend. Her nightmare somehow might be tied to the lighthouse, but she didn't believe in curses, so she doubted that she would believe in this tale of ol' Hyrum. Alice turned to look at her, and Annie dropped her voice to the same dramatic tone Alice had used. "A dark and stormy night."

Alice just wrinkled her nose and went on. "The wind roared along the dirt road, and old Hyrum must have gotten confused. He slipped and fell off the cliff. They found him in the morning, near death on the rocks below."

"Tough old bird to last the night after falling off a cliff," Jim muttered, and Annie laughed again. Alice continued to ignore them.

"His last words were to gasp out the curse. If any kids came to the lighthouse on a stormy night again and touched a single stone of the building, they would be haunted by a host of cliff ghosts and driven mad by morning." Alice finished her story solemnly with a glance at her audience.

"And yet," Annie said, "you survived sneaking up to the lighthouse."

Jim laughed and nudged Alice. "You tempted the curse?"

"I didn't actually touch the stones," Alice said. "I came up with a couple of the guys from around here. It was a dare. I was a sucker for a dare when I was a kid. Anyway, we were caught by the crazy lighthouse keeper who worked here. I thought my folks were going to send me to an all-girls boarding school." Alice caught Annie's incredulous look. "Honestly," she protested, "Mom left boarding-school pamphlets lying around. I tell you, it was psychological warfare. Anyway, sneaking up to the lighthouse on a stormy night has been the thing for teens around here as long as I can remember."

"It's funny how many times these legends involve a crazy lighthouse keeper," Jim said. "I guess the solitude of this kind of work leads to those tales. People assume you have to be crazy to take a job that requires standing alone in a tower during every storm at sea."

"Well, Hyrum may just have been part of the legend," Alice said, "but I can vouch for Murdoch being crazy. You should have heard him ranting at me. I was scared half to death."

Annie smiled at her friend. "Maybe he was worried about you."

"Or maybe he was trying to figure out where to smack me with an ax or something," Alice countered.

Jim burst out laughing. "Well, I thank you for sharing the story in such a vivid way," Jim said. Then his voice grew serious. "Now I just have to find out more about the kids who've died. I'd like to see if either of their deaths tie to the legend."

"Well, the boy doesn't, for sure," Alice said. "I can tell you the particulars of that story sometime, but you can't put it in your book. It has nothing to do with the lighthouse, and I know some people who would be very hurt if it turned into a story told for entertainment."

Jim held up his hands. "I'm not out to hurt anyone. I promise. If you say the boy isn't related to the legend, I accept that. But I still would like to know more about the little girl."

"I didn't know about any little kid dying up here," Alice said.

"I don't remember ever hearing anything about her either," Annie said, "but I may have dreamed about her."

# — 8 —

At Jim's urging, Annie told the bits that she remembered from her dreams. She knew there were children involved, a storm, the lighthouse and the doll. As she struggled to make the shred of memory sound coherent, she decided she just sounded silly. "It's probably nothing," she said lamely.

"I don't know," Jim said, leaning forward to look at her intently with serious gray eyes. "You may have heard about that girl at some time or other, and your memory is making it into a dream. The human mind is an amazing thing."

"Maybe," Annie said doubtfully. "I would rather my memory just made it a memory. The dreams are creepy."

"Of course, it's entirely possible that you're slowly turning into Annie the psychic," Alice said. "In which case, I'm buying you a crystal ball."

"Thanks, pal," Annie said, smiling a little. "Whatever is causing them, I just hope they go away. I can do without the bags under my eyes from lack of sleep."

"Your eyes look right pretty to me," Jim said gallantly.

Annie caught a fleeting frown pass over Alice's face. Her friend was clearly taken with the handsome photographer, and he was certainly charming. Maybe it was time for her to give them some time alone. "You know, I should be getting back," she said, standing and brushing off her crisp cotton pants. "I really should call my daughter about my grandchildren. It was nice to meet you, Mr. Parker. I'll see you at the Hook and Needle meeting, Alice."

At that, Annie turned and hurried off, smiling as she noted that Alice had not protested her sudden departure. "I'll let you know if I learn anything about the girls in your dreams," Jim shouted after her.

She waved her thanks, calling back, "Tell Alice, and she can tell me."

The walk down the long gravel road was almost more treacherous than the walk up. Gravel slipped and slid under Annie's feet, and she had to move slowly to keep her balance. "What must this road be like in the rain?" she murmured.

Finally she made it back to her yard and headed quickly up the back porch. She could hear the phone ringing inside. Boots met her halfway as she raced for the phone and seemed intent on tripping Annie before she could answer it. Despite some odd dance steps they managed together, Annie snagged the phone before the caller gave up. "Hello?" she said breathlessly as she made a face at the cat.

"Mrs. Dawson?" Annie recognized the mellow voice instantly.

"Pastor Mitchell? How nice to hear from you," she said. She slipped into a high-backed Windsor chair by the phone and let the comforting voice of her pastor from Texas flow over her. She asked him about the missionary cupboard and other church programs in which she'd always been involved.

Finally the pastor cleared his throat quietly and said, "I have to confess. I called you because your daughter asked me to. She suggested I talk you into moving back to Texas where ... and I quote ... you belong."

"Ah," Annie said, shaking her head at her daughter's newest plan to get her to give up Grey Gables. "LeeAnn can be single-minded when she wants something. So, are you going to try to talk me into coming back to Texas?"

"No, though I am curious to know what you think about the situation," Pastor Mitchell said. "Where do you feel most called to be?"

Annie sighed. She poured out her heart and her confusion in one long gush. She loved Stony Point and felt a sense of belonging that made her feel right at home. She had made dear friends who were helping her heal after Wayne's death and the loss of Gram in her life. But she couldn't walk away from her life in Texas either.

"I can't bear the idea of never going back to the house Wayne and I shared. Still, I know I can't just ignore the decision forever. I can't just leave the house empty while I think about it for a few years."

"Well, I have an idea," the pastor said slowly. "I'm not trying to talk you into anything, but the church has talked for years about picking up a piece of property for a missionary retreat. There's a real need for a place families on the mission fields can come home to—a place to recharge. It's possible the answer to your problem and ours lies right here."

"You want to buy my house?" Annie asked softly.

"No, the church isn't in a position to buy anything.

The economy has been hard on our congregation. That's what's kept us from acting on this idea years ago. It's very dear to my heart. I was just thinking that if you really feel like you want to make Stony Point your primary home," he explained, "the church could take over the care of your house here. We could pack up your personal things and store them in the attic, but leave most of your belongings untouched. Then, when any mission family needs a place, they could stay in your home. And you could still stay in your home whenever you come back, of course."

Annie blinked at the tears that filled her eyes. Her mother and father had been missionaries, and she loved the idea of offering a shelter for mission families. Still, it felt so strange to think of people coming and going in her home when she wasn't there. Could she let strangers into the home she had shared with Wayne?

"I don't mean for you to make a decision right now," Pastor Mitchell said in response to her silence. "Just think about it and let me know when you know, OK?"

"I will," she said. "I will think about it and pray about it. This may be the answer I've been looking for." She paused for a moment, and then added, "You know the twins' birthday is coming up soon?"

"Yes. LeeAnn told me you are planning to come back for the party," the pastor said. "I believe she was hoping you would stay here once you saw the children again. You should be prepared for a fairly strong campaign on her part."

"I know my daughter well," Annie said, "and I do agree that I need to have made my final decision by then, so that I can stick to it. I'll give you an answer on your proposal as soon as I've made my decision. If I decide to let the church use the house, we can handle any details while I'm there."

The pastor agreed, and their conversation slipped into the comfort zone of catching up on births and weddings in the church. Annie promised that whatever she decided, they would definitely see her in church when she came back for the twins' birthday. "You know I would never miss one of your sermons when I have the opportunity to be there," she said.

"I know," the pastor said. "One thing I could count on every Sunday was the sight of encouraging smiles from you and Wayne whenever I looked out on the congregation. You've been badly missed here. It will be good to see you again, even for a visit."

As she hung up the phone, Annie felt a small glow of hope. She might still not be certain of her decision, but setting a deadline at least meant moving out of this place of limbo. "Whatever I decide," she said quietly to herself, "it will be a relief to feel settled."

At the sound of her voice, Boots padded over and nudged her ankles in a show of support. Annie curled up on the loveseat near the window with a notebook. She decided to make a list of all the reasons she should go back to Texas, and another of all the reasons she should stay in Stony Point. Boots hopped up on her lap and settled down for a nap while she wrote.

For hours, the only sound in the house was the scratch of Annie's pen and birdsong through the window. Finally, a grumble from her stomach reminded her that she hadn't had lunch. She flipped through the filled pages of the notebook and realized she had nearly the same number of things under each heading.

"Well," Annie said, "all I got from that was writer's cramp!"

Boots opened one eye and looked at her. "Nap's over," Annie said, gently shifting the sleepy cat to the loveseat. "I need some lunch."

The cat woke in a flash and followed Annie to the kitchen, more evidence that she spoke perfect English when it came to food.

"What would I do with you if I go back to Texas?" Annie asked the cat as she poured a tall glass of mint tea to go with her freshly made sandwich. "Would you like to become a cowboy kitty?"

Boots glanced up from crunching her kibble, and Annie imagined she saw disapproval on the furry face. "You might like it," Annie said. "You seem like the perfect Southern belle to me."

Annie spent the next couple of days making a tiny crocheted sweater to match the larger one she'd created for Joanna. She thought her granddaughter would love to have a matching sweater for her favorite doll. She was quite proud of how well she adapted the pattern to the much smaller garment.

She was a little surprised when no phone calls came from Alice. Annie realized she was incredibly curious about the possibility of romance for her friend. "I guess I won't be able to complain anymore when the Hook and Needle Club grins at me every time a man speaks to me," she told Boots during one of their afternoon cuddles in the new wicker chair on the porch. "I'm just as bad." But she was glad when club day came around, as now she had a real mystery—the mystery of what was happening with her best friend and the handsome photographer!

She slipped into A Stitch in Time bright and early on Tuesday. Mary Beth looked up in surprise as Annie breezed through the door. "You're first today," she said. "I don't think that's ever happened before. Were you lonely for your dolly?" She patted the rumpled little doll that leaned against the register.

"I'm surprised you kept her out where people can see her," Annie said. "She's a little shabby."

"She's just well-loved," Mary Beth said. "Actually, Kate and I have grown quite attached to her. I do believe Kate has made up a dozen stories of what this little lady has been through. She's become an unofficial store mascot, and we'll miss her when you take her to the library."

"There is something endearing about her," Annie admitted. Thinking of the doll reminded her of her nightmares. She hadn't had one since her phone call with Pastor Mitchell. Maybe having a possible answer to her personal dilemma had chased the bad dreams away. "I had a dream about this little doll a few days ago. It had something to do with Butler's Lighthouse."

"I can't imagine what Butler's Lighthouse could have in common with this sweet little doll," Mary Beth said. "None of the lighthouse keepers ever had children there as far as I know."

Suddenly, Annie laughed. "I bet I know a budding lighthouse researcher who we could ask."

Before Annie could respond to Mary Beth's puzzled look, the bell tinkled over the door, and Alice walked in with Peggy right behind her.

"Ah, I was just talking about you, Alice," Annie said, her voice teasing, "and about how interested you've gotten in lighthouses."

Alice grinned as she walked over and leaned on the counter. "You know me. I'm a huge history buff."

"Since when?" Peggy asked, looking at Alice in surprise.

"Since history became more buff," Annie said.

"All right!" Mary Beth held up her hands. "You two are being way too mysterious, and you know how much I hate being left out. What are you talking about?"

"I'll tell you everything," Alice said, "but let's wait until everyone is here. Otherwise I know you'll make me tell it over and over."

Kate breezed in, huffing a little from rushing. Her dark hair was rumpled from the breeze outside. "Sorry to be late," she said to Mary Beth. "I was longer at Vanessa's doctor than I expected."

"Is Vanessa all right?" Annie asked with concern in her voice.

Kate nodded. "It was just an exam, but there was an insurance mix up. Apparently, Vanessa isn't covered by Harry's insurance anymore, and when I tried to call him, I just got his voice mail. So I had to pay for the visit. It was a bit of a shock."

The women nodded. No one ever knew quite how to respond to Kate's problems with her ex-husband. He clearly loved his daughter, but he could be irresponsible too. It didn't make things easy for Kate. "Let me know if you need a small advance to tide you over," Mary Beth said.

"I'm fine," Kate said. "Just frustrated."

Another jingle at the door drew everyone's attention. Stella swept in with the dignity of an English queen, and Gwen came in right after, dressed in a chic ivory pantsuit with a wide patent-leather belt. Both women were imposing in their own way. Gwen's sense of style always made Annie feel the slightest bit shabby, while Stella's matriarchal attitude subdued everyone around her. The women hurried to their cozy seats. Since the shop was empty of customers, Mary Beth sat with them.

"Now, before we hear the story of Alice's new passion for history," Mary Beth raised an eyebrow when Annie laughed at her choice of words, "I wanted to talk a moment about the doll for the library writing contest. We need to pick which book the doll should represent.

Annie suddenly flashed in her mind to the stack of books in the attic. "I found a really beautiful, old copy of *The Secret Garden* in the attic at Grey Gables," she said. "What if we used that for the theme and gave the winner that lovely old book too? It would tie in with the historical display as well."

"That's an excellent idea!" Mary Beth said. "I remember that story so well. And we could do little knitted stockings for the doll and a nice coat and hat. The story starts in the cold months of early spring, I believe."

"I would love to knit the little stockings," Gwen said. "I have some really fine cream-color yarn that would be just perfect for it."

"I've finished the quilted book cover for Emily's diary, and she loved it," Peggy said. "I could make one for this book. Since the copy from the attic is older, it will give it a nice sprucing up to make it more appealing to the little girl."

"That's a terrific idea," Mary Beth said.

Peggy beamed. "Do you think you could bring the book by The Cup & Saucer so I can get the dimensions?" she asked Annie.

"Of course," Annie said. "I'll bring it by later today or in the morning."

Several of the others made suggestions for additions to the doll's outfit, and soon, everyone had a job. As soon as that was settled, Mary Beth smiled and clapped her hands. "Now on to our mysteries!" she said.

# ~9~

"*I* think we should start with Annie's mystery," Alice said as she settled back in her chair with a tiny baby shoe in her lap. The delicate stitching on the tongue of the shoe was clearly beginning to look like a tiny robin. "I always like her attic mysteries best."

"You're just stalling," Annie teased as she got up to retrieve the doll from the counter and held it up before the group. "I found this lovely little doll in Gram's attic. I don't know who the owner was. Does she look familiar to you, Stella?"

She passed the doll to the older woman. Stella's normally stern face softened as she looked at the doll's sweet expression. "These fabrics are too new to have been Betsy's doll," she said. "And the workmanship isn't nearly good enough to have been made by Betsy for her daughter. I've never seen it before, but it's certainly very sweet."

"She grows on you," Kate said. "I wish we could get her back to her owner. Imagine getting back a childhood treasure like that."

"Well, my ideas for finding her owner began and ended with you, Stella," Annie admitted. "I'm going to put her in the library display. Maybe the owner will walk by and claim her. Wouldn't that be lovely?" Then her smile faded as she thought of her frightening dreams of the girl and the doll.

Could the dreams be more than her overactive imagination? She shook off the gloomy thought and turned to Alice. "OK, my mystery is all done. Tell us about yours."

Alice blushed slightly but otherwise seemed perfectly comfortable. "A photographer is visiting Stony Point and intends to put Butler's Lighthouse in a book on New England lighthouses and legends. I met him, and I'm helping him gather some background information on the lighthouse."

"Has he talked to Liz and Edie at the Historical Society?" Stella asked.

"He has," Alice said, "but they were showing some of the stranger anxiety Stony Point is known for." She paused as Stella sniffed slightly in response to her remark. Stella was often the leader in the campaign to keep strangers at arm's length.

"What do you know about him?" Stella asked pointedly. "Maybe they have good reason to be standoffish. These young paparazzi have no respect for history or tradition."

Annie nearly laughed out loud at Stella's use of *paparazzi*.

"I've looked him up on the Internet, and he's done several very well-received books combining history and photographs," Alice said. "He definitely matches the photo on the author page for those books. Also, he was never paparazzi. When he was younger, he was a war correspondent until he lost his legs in an explosion that brought down the hotel where journalists were staying in Kosovo."

"Oh my!" Annie gasped. Well, that certainly explained the limp.

"I can call the Historical Society," Stella said, her tone softer now. "I'll see if they can be a little more helpful. What did you say the photographer's name was?"

"Jim Parker," Alice said. "He's mostly interested in the legends that tend to spring up around lighthouses. The ghost stories and children's spook tales. I told him about the lighthouse curse as I'd always heard it."

"That's just nonsense," Stella said, her voice back to its normal aristocratic huff. "There certainly should be some real history connected with lighthouses. The book would be much better if it focused on the people saved by lighthouses."

Annie hid a smile by ducking to look at the rag doll in her lap. Stella certainly had an opinion on almost every topic and wasn't the least bit shy about sharing it.

"Apparently people like reading about legends," Alice said. "They're normally a bit of nonsense, though Jim believes they reflect the fears and values of a community. He says you can learn a lot about people by the legends they keep alive."

Stella sniffed and Annie was fairly sure she heard the older woman mutter, "Nonsense."

Alice simply ignored her and continued with her story. "Now, Jim had heard about Cagney's death." The death of the young man was tied to Mary Beth's niece, so it was a touchy subject. Alice paused and turned her eyes to Mary Beth, clearly giving her time to respond.

"That had nothing to do with the lighthouse curse," Mary Beth said tightly. "And I wouldn't like to see the story in a book where it can hurt Amy."

"I'm certain I was able to get Jim to understand that," Alice said. "I told him the basics of that case and that Cagney definitely wasn't trying to defy some lighthouse curse on the night he was murdered. But there is another story he wants to learn more about."

"What story is that?" Mary Beth said warily.

"Apparently a little girl died from a fall near the lighthouse," Alice said. "Jim wasn't sure how long ago, though he is sure it preceded Cagney's death. I promised I would help him track down the details of any deaths of children in the area. Stony Point hasn't seen that many accidents involving young children."

"Thank heavens," Gwen said.

"Anyway," Alice said, "I spent a full day at the newspaper morgue, and I'm certain it couldn't have happened during my childhood or later. But I could use some help tracking further back." She looked hopefully at Annie.

"That's a lot of work to help a stranger," Gwen said, peering at Alice curiously. "What's gotten you so involved in this?"

Alice blushed again. "I wanted to help him see that we're a very friendly community."

"Some of us are friendlier than others," Annie said.

"So," Mary Beth said, "this Jim would be a handsome man?"

"Only if you like bucket loads of charm, dancing gray eyes and a ruggedly handsome silver beard," Alice said. "Otherwise, he's totally ordinary."

"Ah, the mystery is becoming clearer," Mary Beth said as all the women laughed.

"But I don't mind helping with your search," Annie said. "I can check on some of the microfiche at the library. I've gotten really good at research projects since I came to Stony

Point, and I need to go by the library anyway to drop off Miss Dolly and Gram's little tea set."

"Thanks so much," Alice said.

"Anything for the cause of community hospitality," Annie teased.

The rest of the meeting of the Hook and Needle Club passed quickly as everyone caught up on their various projects. As the group began to drift away, Peggy caught Annie by the arm. "Wally is working on the boat for your grandson," she said. "He loved the idea, and since he had a lot of scrap wood in the workshop, he's been spending time every evening working on it. Even Emily has gotten involved. She's been full of suggestions for little details to make it perfect. I suspect Wally might have to create the *HMS Princess* after he finishes this one."

Annie told her she was glad Wally could take on the job. "You don't know what a lifesaver he's being with this," Annie said.

"That's my Wally," Peggy said with a proud smile as she gathered her things and hurried out of the shop.

Annie gathered her own things and noticed Alice was waiting for her. "I've missed you the last couple days," she said.

"You know," Alice said, "you didn't have to leave the other day."

"I think it was definitely a case of 'two's company,'" Annie said. "And you didn't exactly beg me not to go," she added with a smile.

"Sorry about that," Alice said as they waved to Mary Beth and Kate at the counter and headed out onto the street.

"It's just that every guy in town seems to have fallen for you a little bit, and I guess I did feel a tiny bit of the green-eyed monster when Jim was being so charming to you."

"I'm not interested in Jim like that," Annie reminded her, "nor any of the men in Stony Point, for that matter."

"That doesn't always matter," Alice said.

Annie nodded. She did understand. They walked along silently for a moment. Then Annie said, "Since we only have the one lighthouse, you do realize Jim isn't likely to be here that long? His job doesn't let him stay in one place too long."

Alice shrugged. "I know. I'm not looking for Mr. Right, but I enjoy Jim's company. He's smart and funny, and he's had some amazing experiences. Besides, it's been a while since a man seemed to feel it worth his time to be charming to me."

"That says something about the sad state of men in Stony Point," Annie said in mournful tones. Alice burst out laughing and gave her a quick hug before they parted company at the steps of the library.

"Thanks a million for checking on the newspaper stories," she said, giving Annie's hand a quick squeeze.

"Hey, I'm getting good at this research thing. Maybe I'll take up a second career as a journalist or a member of the paparazzi!"

Alice's laugh followed her as she hurried up the steps between the tall white columns. She pushed open the multipaned glass door and hurried into the hushed library. She stopped, as she always did, to breathe in the scent of polished wood, old books, and memories. The library had been one of her favorite spots in Stony Point when she was a girl, though it was a spot she usually visited alone or with Gram. The rambunctious young Alice didn't develop a real love of books until she was much older.

Annie nodded at the framed photo of Josephine Booth, Library Volunteer of the Year for the second year in a row. "Long may you reign," she whispered with a smile.

She hadn't ever actually met the tall older woman in the photo, but had spotted her slipping through the library shelves once or twice. In such a small town, it was almost odd they'd never spoken, especially when she considered how many mystery research projects had brought her to the library. Annie decided that she was definitely going to greet the mysterious Ms. Booth the next time she saw her hurrying around the library on a mission.

Annie smiled as she walked to the circulation desk. Grace Emory stood bent over, studying the circulation computers with a frown. Her short brown hair stood on end in spots as if she'd run her fingers through it a few times in frustration. It gave the small-statured woman an even younger look than usual.

"Computer woes?" Annie asked.

"A bit," Grace said as the frown lines in her face turned upward in a welcoming smile. "The more people who use these circulation computers, the more often they decide to get cranky with us. It's probably user error, but I think I'm going to blame cyber ghosts and gremlins."

Annie chuckled at the idea. Though she had a laptop of her own, Annie was still a little intimidated by computers. She often worried that every time she logged onto the Internet, some kind of computer virus would swoop down and take over her computer like a bad science fiction movie. LeeAnn teased Annie terribly about being so old-fashioned, but for Annie, e-mail couldn't replace the warmth of hearing someone's voice over the phone, and browsing the Internet would never replace the confidence she felt in digging up information at the library or asking questions of real people.

"Are you working on a new mystery?" Grace asked, pulling Annie out of her wandering thoughts.

"Maybe, though this time it isn't *my* mystery," she said. "I'm helping the friend of a friend. I need to go through the microfiche from *The Point* again."

"You're going to end up knowing more about our town newspaper than the editor," Grace said with a smile. "Do you need me to help you with it?"

"No, thanks. I think I finally know my way around the microfiche. Actually, I also need Valerie Duffy. I have some items for the toy display."

"Valerie is back at the reference desk," Grace said, "unless she's in the stacks somewhere. Do you just want to give the things to me? We have a box here under the desk where we're storing the toys as they come in."

Annie handed the doll and tea set to Grace, and the librarian tagged them with Annie's name and contact information before slipping them under the desk. Then Annie headed toward the archway that led into the Reference Room. She glanced around, but didn't see Valerie among the patrons peering into computer screens or poring over the bound reference material.

The microfiche were stored in a tall cabinet of drawers. Each drawer was marked with information about the contents, and over half were taken up with old issues of *The Point*. Since Alice was clearly working backward from present day, Annie decided to work forward from the first days the newspaper began publishing.

Annie sat down in front of the large microfiche reader. She flipped the "on" switch, and the machine made its familiar "thunk" that signaled the beginning of Annie's hunt. She threaded the fiches through the machine and settled in to read the funny old-fashioned script of the first issues.

She read about quilting bees, new businesses and even some articles on possible smugglers on the coast. It was easy to get caught up in the past as she read through the pressing stories of each issue. Some of the stories showed how much times have changed, while others made it clear that the people of Stony Point still have the same core values they'd always had. They loved community events and helping out those in need.

As she scanned each issue, reading whatever caught her eye, Annie realized she knew more about the history of Stony Point than she had ever learned about Brookfield, Texas. All of her mysterious experiences since she'd come back to Grey Gables, and all of her trips to the library had made this town feel more and more like her home. She knew its past and its present. She liked the idea of being here to know its future too.

"I should write that on my list," she murmured as she slid a microfiche from the machine and reached for the next one. She was so deep in her thoughts that she jumped when Valerie's voice came over the speakers, announcing the end of library hours.

# — 10 —

nnie's search had reached the early 1940s, but she still had not found any reports of a child dying near the lighthouse. As she slipped her notes into her purse, she realized that she must be nearing the time the rag doll might have been made.

She had no real evidence to associate the rag doll with the death of the child that Jim told them about, but somehow Annie hadn't really expected to find the little girl in the distant past of Stony Point. And even if the doll and the little lost girl weren't related, Annie thought there was a faint chance she might come across a photo of a little girl with the doll. That would be a quick and convenient end to this attic mystery.

As Annie passed the circulation desk, she stopped to say hi to Valerie. "I dropped off a couple of toys earlier," she said.

"Oh, that's wonderful," Valerie responded. "We've gotten the most interesting collection. Someone even unearthed some cast-iron coin banks. My favorite has a lion that jumps though a hoop to deposit the coin. I'm so glad we're doing this display. I believe the children will enjoy it immensely."

"My contributions aren't as lively as jumping lions," Annie said. "It certainly sounds like you'll have an eye-catching display. When are you going to put it up?"

"Not for another week or so," Valerie said. "We're still getting items every day."

"I'm looking forward to seeing it," Annie said. She walked across the nearly empty library, the tapping of her heels on the floor echoing in the huge room. When she slipped outside, she realized the temperature had fallen with the sun, and she wished she'd worn a cardigan over her square-necked T-shirt. If she was going to be a New Englander, she needed to learn to dress for the quick-changing weather.

The thought of heading home didn't really appeal to her. As she headed down the sidewalk, the lights of The Cup & Saucer cast an inviting warmth. Annie decided she was in the mood for some comfort food, and no one did comfort food better than the diner.

Inside, the smell of gravy wrapped around her, convincing her she'd made the right decision. She looked over the crowded room and spotted Alice and Jim sitting on the same seat in a booth, looking very cozy. Annie noticed that her friend had taken extra care with her appearance, and the deep emerald blouse she wore made her hair blaze.

Jim looked up and noticed her eyes on them. He smiled broadly and waved her over. Annie hesitated, not sure if Alice would be as glad for the interruption, but her friend grinned and waved as well.

Annie slipped through the tables and managed not to bump anyone's chair, which wasn't easy in the busy room. "Come and join us," Alice said. "We haven't really ordered yet. Did you find anything at the library? I told Jim you were joining the hunt."

"I appreciate all the help I can get," Jim said as Annie slipped into the booth seat across from them. "I was showing Alice some of my proof sheets for Butler's Lighthouse. I have some great shots. Now I have to get serious about finding great stories to go with them."

"Did you tell Jim that Stella said she'd try to loosen up the Historical Society?" Annie asked.

"I did. Though the idea of Stella getting someone else to loosen up is definitely unusual," Alice said with a laugh.

"You have to admit, Stella tends to be good at getting people to do what she wants."

"She sounds formidable," Jim said as he slipped his proof sheets into a folder.

"More like terrifying," Annie said. "I was more than a little scared of her when I first moved to Stony Point. But I'm starting to think there might be a tender heart deep inside her."

"Really, *really* deep," Alice added.

Peggy hurried up to their table, her face pink from bustling around. "Sorry to make you wait," she said as she flipped over their coffee cups and filled them from the pot in her hand. "We've been busy all week. It makes me wonder what the real tourist season is going to be like this year." She flashed a dimpled smile at Annie, while cutting her eyes toward Jim and Alice. Annie knew that Peggy must be nearly bursting with the need to talk about the possible romance.

"Alice tells me the meatloaf here is spectacular," Jim

said. "I'd like that, please."

Both Alice and Annie asked for the same, and Peggy hurried away, glancing back several times as if afraid she might miss something interesting.

"I ran though the old issues of *The Point*," Annie said. "All the way up to the early 1940s. I ran across two children who died from pneumonia and one who died of exposure, but at the opposite end of town from the lighthouse." Annie's face clouded slightly as she spoke. "It was a little boy, five years old. He was lost in Myers Woods in the winter."

"Definitely not the kid from the legend," Jim said.

Annie shook her head. "No. I also found the record of a family who died in a house fire. There were two children in that one. And one who died in a car accident. I expect we'll find more car deaths in the newer papers and probably some boating accidents too. Really, it's a bit depressing when you stop and think about it. I hate to think about children dying so young."

Jim nodded, his eyes sympathetic. Then he sighed. "Well, at least we've narrowed the window. Alice read back to the early 1960s, and you've read up to the 1940s. It shouldn't be more than a couple hours to check the rest. I can do that."

"I don't mind finishing," Annie said. "I find the old newspaper fascinating to look through. Plus, I'm coming up on the years where I might see a photo with the old doll from the attic." At Alice's skeptical look, Annie laughed and added, "I know, that would be a crazy coincidence, but I figure, you never know. The newspaper is full of photos from town picnics and events like that." She felt her face warm as Alice's look didn't change.

Jim came to her rescue. "Stranger things have happened."

"Maybe *not* a lot stranger," Alice said wryly.

Soon after, Peggy breezed through the crowd with their plates. As she served, she smiled brightly at Jim. "I hear you're a photographer," she said. "You planning to be in Stony Point long?"

"Hard to say," Jim said. "Lots of interesting things here."

Peggy looked pointedly at Alice. "Seems like," she said cheerily.

As soon as Peggy was swallowed back up in the crowd, Jim burst out laughing. "You were right about folks around here," he said to Alice. "They may not like to answer questions, but they sure like to ask them."

"We combine the rare qualities of being nosy and insular at the same time," Alice said as she cut into the tender meatloaf. "Though I can't imagine you haven't seen that anywhere else in New England."

At that, the conversation drifted to other towns and lighthouses Jim had photographed for the book. From there, it wasn't long before they slid into ghost stories. "A lot of the legends have ghosts," Jim told them. "At the Portsmouth Harbor Lighthouse, it's the lighthouse keeper who haunts the lighthouse tower. Apparently a lot of lighthouse keepers get attached to their jobs and stay on long after they've died. They're seen in the cottages, the lighthouses, and even the cliffs and rocks around the buildings."

He took a sip of his coffee and continued. "In Connecticut, there's a lighthouse that looks like a school out on a big rock in the middle of the water. It's called Ledge Light, and it's apparently haunted by Ernie, another lighthouse keeper who couldn't leave his work."

"And did you see any of these lighthouse-keeping ghosts?" Alice asked skeptically.

"No," Jim admitted, "but I talked to people who said they have. And not all the ghosts are lighthouse keepers. Some of the lighthouses feature lady ghosts too. At the Seguin Island lighthouse, ghosts of the keeper and his wife have both been seen."

"That's a nice romantic story," Annie said.

"Not so much," Jim said. "Apparently they hang around because the keeper killed his wife with an ax and then flung himself from the cliff." Jim saw Annie shudder and moved quickly on to a less gruesome story. "Out on Ram Island, there's a ghostly woman in white who shows up when a bad storm is coming. Like the Butler's Lighthouse legend, storms are common elements in these stories."

"I don't suppose you saw the woman in white either?" Alice asked.

"No, but I've been in some of these old lighthouses after dark," Jim said. "They're lonely places and pretty spooky. I could see how these legends spring up." Then he grinned at Alice. "Interestingly enough, a red-haired lady ghost apparently visits the lighthouse keeper's cottage at one of the Maine lighthouses I've visited. I was particularly interested in that one, but then I came out here to visit the Butler's Lighthouse and met an even more interesting red-haired lady."

"Is that right?" Alice said, grinning at Jim's flirting.

Annie wondered if she should excuse herself and leave her friends alone. She still wasn't eager to go out in the cold, but if they wanted to be alone, she didn't want to interrupt.

Jim finally looked back at Annie and said, "It's actually fairly rare to have children in lighthouse ghost stories."

"The legend also focuses less on the ghosts than on what can happen to living people," Annie said. "The victims are children, and the lighthouse keeper was some kind of witch—or would he be a warlock? Anyway, he cursed the kids."

"Right—it's more of a traditional cautionary tale," Jim said. "If we look at legends and folktales all over the world, we find lots of examples of cautionary tales. Here the story cautions against traveling a dangerous stretch of road at night during storms, but some legends warn against bad things that can happen if you're mean to strangers, or if you steal or are greedy. Cautionary tales are often older than the more gruesome ghost stories like the ax-wielding lighthouse keeper. That's why I want to be sure to include this legend. And if I can track down anyone whose death was even a little like the story, well, that's going to add to the chill."

Annie frowned slightly. She wasn't sure the tragic death of a child was really something to be used to sell books. Jim seemed to sense her discomfort because he moved on to talking about the unusual styles of the lighthouses, and the rest of the meal passed pleasantly.

Annie decided she liked how comfortable Jim seemed

with himself. Clearly he'd had more than his share of grief in life, but nothing in his attitude reflected either anger or self-pity. She found herself envying his contentment, and she hoped his relationship with Alice didn't end up hurting either one of them.

Peggy appeared like magic at their table as they finished the meal. Alice and Jim ordered pie, but Annie decided to head for home before she wore out her welcome with her friend. She paid her bill and slipped out of the booth.

"I'll finish up that research tomorrow and let Alice know if I find anything," Annie said.

"You know," Jim replied, "you could call me directly. I'm staying at the Maplehurst Inn. If I'm not there, you can leave a message."

"I'll call both of you so no one feels left out," Annie said brightly, making Jim and Alice chuckle. Then she headed for the door.

Peggy caught her just before she slipped out. "Don't forget that copy of *The Secret Garden*," she said. "I could get right on the cover tomorrow night that way. With Emily focused on helping Wally with your grandson's boat, I'm getting a lot more stitching done in the evening."

"I'm glad my project has done so much good," Annie said with a laugh. "I'll definitely set the book out before I go to bed," Annie promised. "That way I can't forget."

"Great," Peggy said. She looked pointedly at the booth where Alice and Jim had their heads together. "They make a cute couple. Do you suppose he'll stay?"

Annie sighed. "I doubt it, but I like him. I just hope Alice doesn't get her heart broken."

"It's happened before," Peggy said.

"Which is why I hope it doesn't happen again," Annie said. "But I think Jim is a nice guy. And I'm trying to keep my list of things to worry about under a hundred per day."

With that she excused herself and headed for home.

~ 11 ~

Grey Gables was dark as Annie pulled up since she hadn't expected to spend quite so long in town. Annie sat quietly in her Malibu and stared up at the old Victorian. The wide front porch that looked so welcoming in the daylight now shadowed the front door ominously, and the oversized wicker furniture offered plenty of spots for an intruder to crouch and hide.

Annie gave herself a little mental shake. She loved Gram's house, but it was hard to be there alone sometimes, especially after dark. Finally, Annie took a deep steadying breath and swung open the car door.

All of Jim's ghost stories had left her a little jumpy. She forced a nervous laugh as she told herself that Grey Gables hadn't had a prowler in weeks and had never had a ghost as far as she knew. Betsy Holden wouldn't have put up with a ghost! She wasn't someone who believed in such things. Surely one mysterious little doll wouldn't bring anyone skulking around this time.

Boots greeted her with a chorus of indignant meows. This was such completely normal behavior for the spoiled cat that Annie felt the tension drain out of her.

"It's nice to be missed," she told the cat as it threaded through her legs and bumped against her shins. Annie checked her answering machine and was glad to see she hadn't missed any calls.

"Book!" she said, remembering her promise to Peggy. She felt the tiniest thrill of nerves at the thought of tackling the dark attic at night, but she knew exactly where the books were, so she'd just grab them and get it over with. She trekked upstairs, pausing long enough to shove Boots into her bedroom, despite the cat's outraged protests. "I'm jumpy enough without you playing ghost this evening," Annie called through the door.

She headed up the attic stairs, glad for the hours she'd spent cleaning and organizing. It made reaching the maple dressing table much easier. Annie wove her way through quickly, focusing on her goal and trying not to notice how the single light made weird twisted shadows creep across the floor. Rather than sort through the books, Annie just grabbed them all and retraced her steps. Again she paused at the bedroom door, opening it and releasing the furious ball of fur. She headed downstairs to the kitchen; Boots stalked after her.

Annie turned the books to look at the spines: *The Outdoor Girls of Foaming Falls, Nancy Drew and the Mystery of the Old Clock, Anne of Green Gables, The Secret Garden* and one well-worn book with no title on the spine. Annie recognized it as the book that had been wedged behind the doll box.

She opened it and discovered it was a journal. The flyleaf was covered in cheerful script, and the writer had dotted each i with little smiles, hearts, or flowers. The owner had also decorated the border of the page with simple doodles of flowers and swirls. It gave the page a cheerful confusion.

Annie gasped as she read the admonishment written there: "This book belongs to Judy Holden. The treasures and secrets inside are not to be read by strangers under any circumstances or else!!!" She smiled at the insistence reflected in the row of exclamation points at the end.

She'd found her mother's journal. She flipped through a few pages and a folded sheet of paper fell out. Annie picked it up and unfolded it carefully. It was an award certificate for learning the most Bible verses for the year 1955 in a church youth group. Annie remembered how often her mother had quoted from the Bible in her everyday life, her head stuffed with references.

"Memory is sometimes the only Bible a missionary can carry into a really dangerous area," her mother had once told her. "There's nothing more valuable you can put in your head than scripture. Put the words in there now, and they'll come to you when you need them."

Annie had tried to memorize Scripture, but really only knew a handful of Psalms and a scattering of New Testament verses. Annie was proud of her mother's commitment to the mission field, but it wasn't something they could share. There were times when Annie felt such a crushing sense of loss. Really, she'd known Gram better than she'd known her own parents. They had traveled to such dangerous places sometimes, places they didn't want to take a young girl. So Annie spent her summers with Gram and much of her school year with her dad's sister Susan in Texas.

She loved Aunt Susan too, but somehow the longing for her own parents overshadowed much of her childhood.

It was as though nearly her whole young life was spent waiting—waiting for her parents to come home, and even waiting for the chance to really know them at all. And then they'd both died so young. Annie sighed and slipped the paper back into the journal.

She carried it into the bedroom and changed for bed. Then she slipped between the crisp cotton sheets and opened the book again. She found other bits tucked between the pages. Two black-and-white photos showed her mother dressed in long skirts that skimmed her rolled-down bobby socks. Judy Holden smiled stiffly at the camera, not showing her teeth. She had so few pictures like this of her mother as a young girl. Either her mother hadn't cared much for photos, or it simply had been hard to slow her down enough to take her picture. Annie remembered Gram telling her that Judy was always rushing off to one adventure or another.

Annie tried to picture that kind of excitement as she looked at the girl in the photos. She ran a finger over the high ponytail her mother wore in the photos. The mother she remembered had always kept her hair short, saying it made life easier.

Annie remembered asking her mother why short hair was easier. "Sometimes we go to places where ... " her mother paused, as if looking for a gentle way to say what she meant, " ... where not everyone is able to keep bedding and such clean. And it helps if you can reach your scalp easily."

Annie still looked confused, so her mother added, "I've had lice about five times now, and bedbug bites even more often."

When Annie wrinkled her nose, her mom had patted her arm. "Sometimes there are more important things to worry about than a few fleas or lice."

That little talk had left Annie itchy for the rest of the day. How different her practical mother seemed from the girl in the photos with her saddle shoes and ponytail. "I wish I had known you better," she whispered as she looked into the eyes of the girl squinting at the camera. Her eyes misted with tears.

Annie could see that she looked a lot like her mother. She had the same fine blond hair and pointed chin, features she shared with her own daughter LeeAnn. All three shared the same fine bone structure, an inheritance from Betsy Holden. But she suspected the women inside had little in common. Though Annie cared about missionaries, she had never felt the call to go overseas. In that, she and her mother were very different.

Annie turned back to the journal, flipping pages slowly to see what else might be tucked inside. She found a four-leaf clover as well as violets and other wild flowers pressed between the pages. Then the book fell open to a spot where a tightly folded piece of paper with careful square handwriting was tucked deeply into the crack of the binding. The note wasn't signed, but the writer declared his admiration for Judy in an awkward poem:

*Your hair is gold like the sun.*
*Your eyes are blue as the sea in spring.*
*If you liked me as I like you,*
*I know my heart would sing.*

"Wow, that boy had it bad," Annie said, turning to

speak to the photo of her mother. "I wish you were here to tell me about him."

She wondered if maybe her mother had written about her mystery beau in the journal, so Annie turned to the first page of script and began to read:

*June 25th. The Wild Jays had a picnic on the beach today. Jenny went on and on about Butler's Lighthouse again. She has been obsessed with the place ever since Jo told her about the legend. Now, whenever we get together, she begs for new ghost stories. I think Jo is just making things up half the time. She's really good at it. By the time she finished one about a ghost ship filled with blood-soaked pirates, I had goose bumps on my goose bumps, and Jenny had practically hugged all the stuffing out of poor Matilda.*

Annie stared at the page in shock. Was Matilda the old rag doll she'd found in the attic? If so, how did it end up in the attic of Grey Gables? Annie also thought about the uncanny connections between her mother's journal and her own nightmares. The three girls. The lighthouse that apparently frightened and fascinated the youngest girl. The doll.

How could Annie be dreaming about these girls when this was the first she knew of their existence? Had her mother told her about them at some point or other, and her dream was turning the memory into pictures for her?

Judy had never been one to tell stories of her childhood. Her eyes were always on the future and the next task to be done. Annie had admired her mother for that dedication to finding a need that she could fill, but it meant that she didn't know much about her mother's childhood. Gram talked about it sometimes, especially when Annie did something that reminded her grandmother of Judy. Could that be where she heard of this story? Or maybe her mother had told her when she was really little, and the memory could only be accessed in her sleep?

Annie didn't know the answer, but suddenly the thought of sleep was very appealing. She felt like she'd been handed an almost overwhelming number of insights into her mother, and just trying to sort them out in her head was exhausting. Boots hopped up on the bed and climbed onto the open book in Annie's lap, pointedly flopping down on it.

"OK, Boots," Annie said. "I can take a hint. Sleep now, read tomorrow!" She slipped the book out from under the boneless cat and laid it to one side. Then she turned off the light and settled down, the promise of learning more about her mom giving her a small glow of warmth as she slipped into sleep.

It turned out to be one of those nights that seemed to pass in an instant. She closed her eyes on the night and opened them seemingly just after that to find morning sun on her face. She was happy for another night without a nightmare as she'd been a little worried the book would trigger one.

Annie retrieved her mother's journal and carried it with her to the kitchen. She settled at the table with a cup of coffee and a muffin, opening the book to read the next entry.

*July 5th. Jenny now talks about nothing but the lighthouse. I think the only thing that is going to get her to stop bugging us is if we finally get to go inside. We've decided to ask the new lighthouse keeper to give us a tour. I would be scared to death to ask, because everyone knows Mr. Murdoch hates kids, but Jo isn't afraid of anything. She says she's going to march right up there tomorrow. Of course, that's going to mean me marching with her. Jo and I are a team! Jo says I have to come anyway, because I can charm the birds from the trees. So between Jo's courage and my way with people, we just might get our tour. The next time I write, I'll be telling you all about our tour. We're not going to take Jenny until the tour is a sure thing. She may love to talk about the lighthouse, but I don't think she'll be brave enough for more than one visit.*

Annie smiled at the lighthouse keeper's name and wondered if it was the same man who caught Alice and her friends. If so, the man had stayed on long enough to grow old in the job without getting a bit nicer to kids.

In the journal entries, her mom and Jo sounded so much like Annie and Alice as kids. Alice was the one who never saw a dare she could pass up, and Annie was the one who talked them out of trouble after one of Alice's wild ideas went totally off course.

Annie flipped to the next page in the book and saw her mom had dotted all the i's in this entry with frowning faces. The entry was short:

*July 6th. Mr. Murdoch is such a grouch!! He wouldn't even let us ask about a tour and just started yelling when we knocked on the door! He even threatened to sic his monster dog on us!!!! Jo says she's not afraid of Mr. Murdoch or the dog, or even the curse. Sometimes I worry when Jo gets this worked up. Why couldn't that grouchy man just let us have a tour?*

Annie felt a stir of unease at the entry. Sure, her mother had sounded angry, but worried too. What had her best friend's wild ideas gotten them into? She started to turn the page when the ringing of the phone made her jump.

When she picked up the phone, she was delighted to hear the voice of her daughter. "You won't believe what I was reading when you called," Annie said.

"Hmmm … *Snagging the Sexy Senior*?" LeeAnn asked.

"You made that title up!"

"No, really," LeeAnn said, laughing. "I saw it on the cover of a magazine in a bookstore in Dallas. Since it's about the last thing I could imagine you reading, I thought I'd guess that."

"Actually I was reading something much better. I found a journal that belonged to your grandmother when she was a girl. So far, it's very mysterious. It even has a love note tucked inside from some mysterious beau who wrote poetry."

"Poetry?" LeeAnn said. "Poor Herb tried to write a poem for me once. He was so stuck for a rhyme for Lee-Ann that he settled for 'be tan.' I guess you should have given me an easier name."

"Well, your grandmother's beau didn't even try to rhyme Judy," Annie said. "I'm still hoping for clues to who it was. I know she didn't meet your grandfather until she was in her late teens." Annie went on to tell LeeAnn about the old rag doll and the connection to her mom's friends who called themselves the "Wild Jays."

For the first time, LeeAnn showed real interest in one of Annie's mysteries. "You should bring the journal when you come home for the party," she said. "I'd love to read it.

Do you think you can find the rest of the Wild Jays? After all, Grandmother wouldn't be that old now if she had lived. Her friends might still live there in Stony Point."

"The journal hasn't had a lot of clues as to whom they could be so far," Annie said as she ran a finger along the spine of the journal. "But I've only just started reading it. It would be great to meet someone who actually knew Mom when they were kids. I could learn so much."

"Well, let me know what you find out," LeeAnn said. "We can have long, long talks about it when you finally come home."

"That reminds me," Annie said, her voice turning stern, "I don't think it was appropriate for you to ask Pastor Mitchell to talk me into coming back to Brookfield to live."

"It wasn't exactly like that," LeeAnn protested, her voice sputtering a bit.

"Really? What was it like then?"

"Well, it was mostly like that," LeeAnn admitted. "But you're missing so much, Mom. The twins are changing every day, and they want to see their grandmother. And I would like to spend some time with my mom."

Annie sighed. She decided not to remind LeeAnn of how little time they managed to spend together when she lived there in Brookfield. LeeAnn was always rushing from one place to another, and they still visited on the phone far more than they did in person. Would Annie be going back to feeling like a chore on LeeAnn's to-do list if she moved back to Texas?

The phone call wound down with Annie firmly telling LeeAnn that she would appreciate no more schemes to get her back to Texas. "I'll be there for the twins' party," Annie said. "And I promise to have a firm decision by then. You are right about one thing. It's time I settled on where I belong. This being in limbo hasn't been good."

"I'm glad you're finally seeing that," LeeAnn said, her own voice turning firm this time.

# ～12～

fter she finished on the phone, Annie hurried to get ready for her trip into town since the combination of journal reading and chatting with LeeAnn had her running late. She grabbed a sage green jersey cardigan from Gram's closet, remembering how chilly she'd gotten the day before. There was no telling how long she might be out today. She was certainly a much busier person since she had come to Stony Point.

She picked up *The Secret Garden* and slipped it into her purse, and then rushed out to her car. As she drove, she made a little mental to-do list: drop off book, finish library research and check with Mary Beth to see if there was anything she could do to help with the library event. To that list, Annie considered adding a quick trip to her lawyer's office. She'd like to talk with him about any legalities she ought to consider if she decided to take Pastor Mitchell up on his idea of using the Brookfield house as a missionary retreat.

Her to-do list was derailed at her first stop. As she hurried into The Cup & Saucer, Ian stood just inside the door. "What a wonderful surprise," Ian said. "Will you save a friend from a lonely breakfast?"

The muffin Annie had eaten at home seemed to have left plenty of room in her appetite. "That would be nice," she agreed.

Peggy swooped down on them and filled their coffee cups. Annie handed her the book. "Thanks, so much," she said. "I was sketching a plan for the quilting just last night."

"I'm sure it will be beautiful," Annie said.

"Will you be having your usual, Mr. Mayor?" Peggy asked.

"No, I'm breaking out of my rut. Bring me pancakes," he said "and bacon."

Annie and Peggy both smiled at Ian's attempt at bold change from his usual egg and toast. "I think I'll try Ian's usual egg and toast," Annie said. "We don't want the cook getting out of practice making the mayor's complicated breakfast."

Peggy's eyes danced with laughter as she nodded, and then cut her eyes toward the kitchen before leaning close to the table and whispering. "Alice and her gentleman friend were in here until closing time last night."

"They must love your coffee," Annie said mildly. She had no intention of gossiping about Alice. She loved Peggy dearly but was fully aware that anything she said would be all over town by lunchtime. Alice might be used to the small town's lightning-fast gossip chain, but Annie didn't want to contribute to it more than she had to.

"It is great coffee," Ian chimed in as he looked from one woman to the other. Peggy clearly wasn't offended in the least by Annie's redirection as she winked at Annie and headed off to the next table.

Ian smiled at Annie over his coffee cup. "I assume Alice is seeing someone new?"

"You mean there is something happening in Stony Point that the mayor doesn't know about?" Annie asked in mock shock. "I do believe that's a first."

"Everyone has an off day."

Annie laughed. "Have you met Jim Parker, the photographer researching Butler's Lighthouse?"

Ian shook his head. "Charlotte mentioned him though. I believe he's been visiting the Historical Society, and the ladies there don't totally approve of him. Apparently Liz felt his clothes were shabby, and he has a scruffy beard. Charlotte made him sound like a lost hippy who might be up to all manner of nefarious deeds."

Annie laughed at the description. "Actually he has more of a grizzled sea-captain look, I think. Between Peggy and your secretary, I'm starting to understand why you're always so well informed."

"I could say a mayor needs to understand what goes on in his town," Ian quipped, "but I have to admit, I listen to Charlotte out of self-defense. When she comes in with a story to tell, it's just not safe to refuse to listen. She may work for me, but I'm not confused enough to think I'm her *boss*."

Annie nearly laughed out loud. She had thought Ian's secretary only scared *her*. It was good to know Charlotte made Ian a little nervous too. "Just out of curiosity," Annie said, "why did you hire her?"

"I inherited her from the previous mayor," Ian said. "I think she might have come with the original building. No one has quite the courage to replace her."

"I'm getting a whole new vision of you, Mr. Mayor."

"I'm predictable and easily terrified," Ian said. "Now you know all my secrets."

"Your secrets are safe with me," she said.

"I believe that completely." Ian sipped from his coffee

mug, then asked: "So, back to our original topic—is this Jim Parker interested in Alice?"

"They seem to be mutually interested in one another," Annie said.

"What do you think of him?" Ian asked. "I like Alice, but she hasn't always shown the best judgment about men."

Annie thought about her own record as a judge of character, especially the incident of being both charmed and terrified by a slick crook who'd come to Stony Point months ago. Were her own instincts any better than Alice's?

She sighed. "I don't know. I like him, and he seems sincere. Alice was smart enough to check up on him, but I don't get the feeling he's planning to stay in the area long. Alice said she understands that, but ... " Annie shrugged.

"What you know and what you feel aren't always in sync," Ian finished for her.

"Not always," Annie agreed. "At any rate, Jim Parker is interested in the lighthouse legend, and whether it ever actually claimed any victims."

"You mean the lighthouse keeper's curse?" Ian asked incredulously. "That's just a story to scare kids and drive the police crazy."

"He thinks a little girl may have died near the lighthouse," Annie said. "It might be connected to the legend somehow. Maybe a little girl from around the time my mother was young?"

"Your mother?" Ian said. "I never met Judy Spencer, and I'm not quite old enough to have known her when she was a Holden. Didn't she marry a missionary who visited here to talk about his trips?"

Annie nodded. "Dad was only a little older than Mom. His parents were missionaries before him, and he never considered anything else. My mom always knew she wanted to help people, but I'm not sure how much she'd thought about being a missionary before she met Dad. In fact, I've never known a lot about her at all, but I'm starting to learn."

"Oh, how's that?" Ian asked.

Annie smiled and leaned forward eagerly, her face lighting up. "I found a journal from when she was a kid. She was one of the Wild Jays I told you about."

"So it was her doll?" Ian asked.

Annie shook her head. "No, I think it belonged to another girl. But I still feel like I'm getting closer. And it's wonderful to get that peek into my mother's life as a young girl."

"Anything I can do to help?" Ian asked.

"No," Annie said, "but if something comes up, I'll let you know."

They finished their breakfast soon after and left the diner together. Ian reminded Annie to call if she needed any help. Then he crossed Main Street to head toward Town Square. Annie watched him for a moment, thinking how very lucky she was to have made such good friends.

Then she mentally reviewed her to-do list. Did she want to head up the street to the library or down the street to check with Mary Beth about the crafts program? The day was too beautiful to shut herself away in the Reference Room yet, so she decided to check with Mary Beth first.

She had reached A Stitch in Time when she heard her name shouted from across the street. Alice and Jim were coming out of Malone's Hardware. "Annie," Alice shouted again. "Come and join us on our adventure!"

Annie smiled and crossed the street, thinking Alice's dressy clothes didn't look like adventure wear to her. Alice looked especially chic in a pair of perfectly tailored white slacks with a black silk tee that draped softly at the neckline. A wide black belt and lightweight cardigan in thin black and white stripes made Alice's hair the only burst of color, drawing extra attention to it.

"What kind of adventure do you have in mind?" Annie asked.

"We're entering the cave of the dragon ladies," Alice said.

Jim laughed. "Actually we're going to visit the Historical Society again to see if your friend has softened them up."

Annie looked over Jim's well-worn jeans. His shirt was a soft blue and obviously new. She wondered if Alice had a hand in sprucing him up since his hair looked almost tame. "You look nice," she said.

"It's Alice's intervention," Jim said, and Alice caught his arm just before he could run a nervous hand through his hair. "She's helping me look presentable to see if that helps. I tend to feel overdressed if I don't have enough wrinkles in my clothes."

"I think you look very presentable," Annie said. "But do you really want me along?"

"Absolutely," Alice said, linking her arm through Annie's and towing her along as they headed toward Alice's convertible. "They adore you at the Historical Society ever since you found that unknown Betsy Original in the attic, not to mention that map."

"I don't know about that," Annie said, "but I'm happy to help however I can. I still think my mystery might have some overlap with yours."

"Well, I hope you aren't disappointed in that," Alice said as they neared the car. "I'm glad you're willing to come. How can anyone be mean to Annie Dawson?"

"As I remember, some of the folks here have had no trouble at all with that," Annie said.

"All horrible misunderstandings," Alice said, continuing to tow her friend along.

"But this is going to put off my finishing that research at the library."

"First things first," Alice said. "We're off to do battle with dragons!"

# — 13 —

Annie had actually never been to the old Historical Society building. Stella Brickson had told the group months ago that the society hoped eventually to transfer everything to a larger building adjacent to the new Cultural Center, but the group stayed so busy they had not gotten much moved yet.

Alice found an empty parking spot near the old brick building. Like many New England structures, it looked a bit like someone had built a normal brick building, and then squished it from both sides until it looked abnormally tall and narrow. The windows mirrored the structure of the building, and the door to the street had a small white sign that said "Stony Point Historical Society."

As they climbed out of the car, Annie smiled at Jim's wind-tousled hair. Riding with the top down on the convertible had definitely undone his efforts to look refined. Alice paused to fuss over him a moment, but finally gave in with a shrug when the heavy lock of gray hair fell over his forehead for the third time. "I give up," Alice said. "Your natural ruggedness defeats me."

"We'll just hope for the best," Jim said.

Alice led the group into the building with all the determination of an explorer conquering a mountain. The door opened to a long, dark hall with open doorways on either side.

Each doorway had a sign indicating its contents, including such unusual labels as "Town Ephemera" and "Whaling and War Artifacts."

"Hello?" Annie called softly. "Is anyone here?"

A willowy older woman, who Annie recognized as Liz Booth, president of the Historical Society, stepped out of one of the far rooms and smiled warmly at Annie. She had close-cropped white hair that looked fine as fledgling down. She wore corded slacks in a vintage avocado color and a blouse constructed from a wild collection of fabrics in reds, blues and greens. The chocolate-colored velvet collar of the blouse matched the woman's brushed-suede flats.

"Hi, Annie! It's nice to see you again," Liz said, warmly. "May I help you with anything?" She then appeared to catch sight of Jim as he limped through the door behind Annie and Alice. Her smile stayed on her face but looked strained around the edges.

"Hello, Liz," Annie said. "We were hoping you could answer some questions we had about Butler's Lighthouse."

"Of course," Liz replied. "Please, come back here where we can sit comfortably."

"Thanks," Annie said as she followed Liz back into the room she'd stepped from. The room was more brightly lit than the hall, the tall windows letting in the morning light. The sparsely furnished room held a battered old oak desk pushed under the windows and a leather loveseat and several high-backed chairs in a small grouping around a low table.

The older woman sat perched on the edge of one of the chairs. Alice and Jim settled onto the loveseat, and Annie took another chair in the circle. Liz looked pointedly at Jim.

"Stella Brickson spoke to us about you and your research," she said. "I still am not interested in seeing private information about Stony Point families in a book, but I will be happy to help you with information on the Butler's Lighthouse legend."

"Actually, I have a question," Alice said, "and I've always wanted to ask someone. Why was the lighthouse keeper so mean when I was a kid?"

Liz smiled slightly. "You must mean Matthew Murdoch. His is a very sad story, but it might be interesting for your book." She cut her eyes to Jim.

"Do you mind if I record this?" he asked, fishing a small digital recorder from his shirt pocket.

"No, I don't mind," she said, "but keep in mind that I'm working from memory here, though I can show you all the documentation we have to back it up."

"Thank you," Jim said. "I suspect your memory is impressive."

Liz smiled at that, and Annie noticed some of the strain had slipped from her face.

"Matthew Murdock was a ship's captain before he became a lighthouse keeper," Liz began, her voice settling into a nice storytelling lilt. "He had a fishing vessel that sailed out of Stonington in Connecticut. Normally each fishing trip lasted from three to eight days. His boat was a dragger, meaning he used nets for bottom fishing. He was rather young to captain his own ship, but it was a family business, and I understand he was very competent."

"And cranky," Alice muttered.

"That came later, I think," Liz said, smiling slightly at Alice's grumble. "Matthew was married, and they had a young son. The little boy adored his father and often begged to go out on the fishing boat. Finally, Matthew agreed. The day seemed clear and bright, but we know how quickly weather can change in New England on the coast."

All three listeners nodded in unison, already caught up in the story.

"The weather turned violent suddenly. Captain Murdoch sent his wife and son below when waves began washing over the side of the ship. He feared they would be swept away, and he trusted in his ability to get them safely home. The wind and waves pushed the fishing boat even further south, well past where they wanted to be and toward a rocky shore. A lighthouse warned boats away from that shore, but it wasn't lit on that stormy night. Rumor says the lighthouse keeper drank too much, passed out and let the light go out. The boat ran upon a rock and sunk so quickly that the captain couldn't get to his wife and child. They alone drowned, while the captain and crew survived."

"How horrible!" Annie whispered, thinking of the frightened woman, trapped below the deck in the dark as the water rushed in. For a moment her mind turned to Wally Carson and his desperate longing to captain his own ship, and her imagination replaced the faceless woman and child with the faces of Peggy and Emily. She pushed the image away quickly, but it made her shiver.

"Many say it drove Matthew mad," Liz went on, her voice turning a bit mournful. "He never returned to the sea and took up the job here as lighthouse keeper, vowing that his light would never go out. He rarely left the lighthouse for any reason and half-starved himself and his dog for fear of the light going out when he was in town getting supplies."

"Poor man," Annie said kindly.

"Poor dog," Alice grumbled.

"Butler's Lighthouse saved a number of ships during Murdoch's years of keeping," Liz said. "I believe he received a commendation for his work more than once."

"What happened to the lighthouse keeper who let his light go out?" Jim asked.

"He was fired, of course," Liz said. "And he might have been tried for his negligence, but he disappeared. Some whispered that Murdoch killed him, but that's just gossip. There was never evidence of something like that."

"I could picture Old Man Murdoch killing someone," Alice said. "He was mean."

"He was still a young man when he took over here," Liz continued. "He never mixed much with the local people, though that might have been partly from his fear of ever leaving the lighthouse. People say he was especially upset whenever he saw children in danger, even danger they brought on themselves." She looked pointedly at Alice with that remark.

"So he would have been very upset by children out in a storm," Jim said.

"Upset," Alice grumbled. "Try crazy."

"I believe he would have been," Liz said. "I never actually met Mr. Murdoch as I wasn't yet involved with the Historical Society when he died, though my mother was. She always felt Murdoch was far more sad than scary."

"How did he die?" Jim asked.

"He had a heart attack," she said. "He was found in the lighthouse keeper's cottage." Then she turned to Annie. "It was actually your grandmother who alerted authorities that something must be wrong. The keeper's dog came down and scratched at her door. Since that dog never ever left the lighthouse property, Betsy immediately called the police, and they found poor Matthew in the cottage. He would have been glad to know he was found before the light could go out."

"Gram never told me about that," Annie said.

"You would probably have been a young mother then," Liz said. "Besides, Betsy Holden always preferred to focus on the good news of life."

"That she did," Annie agreed. Gram never failed to tell her about Stony Point celebrations or good news about the people she knew. Gram was no Pollyanna, but she chose to focus on life.

"I admired that about her," Liz said, "but I believe that the sad stories of history are worth telling too, or else the people who struggled and suffered are forgotten. There is an old saying that a man isn't truly dead as long as someone remembers him. So, in a way, our job here at the Historical Society is to keep memories alive—good ones and bad ones."

"There's another sad memory I'd like to know more about," Jim said. "It's the story of the child who died near the lighthouse. I believe it's tied to the lighthouse curse."

"The lighthouse curse is a simple cautionary tale," Liz said. "It's the kind of legend you hear in connection with many dangerous places. Do you know the story?"

Jim nodded. "I've heard it from Alice and a few others around town. All basically tell the same story of a lighthouse keeper tormented by the local children who curses them with his dying breath should they ever touch the lighthouse on a stormy night."

"We have no reason to believe such a man ever existed.

Mr. Murdoch isn't the first keeper to die at the lighthouse, but all of them seem to have been well-liked. There is no evidence of a crazed keeper tormented by local children." Liz shook her head sadly. "The story is meant to keep children safe, obviously. But too often such stories do just the opposite. They tempt the reckless." Again she looked at Alice.

Alice colored slightly. "I was young," she protested.

Then Liz's face broke into a sheepish smile. "Actually, I tried it too, but I got cold feet halfway up that dark road." Then she pointed a finger at Jim. "That better not turn up in your book."

"It won't," he said, holding his hands up in surrender, "but can you tell me about the child who didn't survive that curse?"

"No," Liz said.

"No, you can't?" Jim asked. "Or no, you won't?"

Liz sat forward on her chair and folded her hands in her lap. "I'm truly not trying to be difficult, Mr. Parker, but you're asking for a story that is very personal and private. I am not someone who believes the dead can be hurt by stories, but I do know that the living can be devastated. This is not a story I *can* share with you. I would have to get the permission of someone I would never even dare approach about it."

Jim nodded. "I can respect that. Then we've probably taken all of your time we need to for today." He stood and smiled at Liz. "You've been a great help."

"Then I'm glad," Liz said. "Since Stella told me that you would almost certainly be coming by, I also put a packet together for you of all the things we have here at the Society that relate to the lighthouse. I made photocopies." She walked to the desk and picked up a thick folder bound by rubber bands. She handed it to Jim. "Will you be in Stony Point much longer?"

"I'm afraid not," Jim said, tucking the folder under his arm. "I have one last series of photos I want to shoot, but I'll probably be leaving in the next few days. Still, I know this will be a huge help." He tapped the edge of the bulging folder with a finger.

"I hope it will."

Annie watched her friend's face to see if Jim's impending departure was news to Alice, but she didn't seem surprised. Annie just hoped she was prepared.

Before they could excuse themselves, Liz asked Alice a question about a recent Divine Décor order. Annie smiled at that. Her friend was amazingly successful with her decorating and jewelry parties, more than Annie would have expected considering Stony Point was a relatively small town. Of course, Annie had picked up more than a few things from Alice herself. The Divine Decor style seemed to work well with the stately older homes around the area as they had a touch of the vintage about them.

Finally, Alice broke away, and they headed out to the parking lot. "I'm sorry that wasn't more successful," she said to Jim.

"That's OK," Jim said, smiling ruefully. "In my business, you do a lot of fishing for facts. Sometimes you land something big, and sometimes it gets away. I think the story of the mad lighthouse keeper will be a nice addition though."

"That was such a sad story," Annie said.

"Yes, it was," Alice agreed as she fished in her purse for her keys. "I can almost forgive him for being such a grouch. I'm still trying to reconcile the crazy guy screaming at me with the image of a tragic young husband and father."

"You know, Ian asked me if I wanted to go whale watching on his brother's lobster ship sometime," Annie said. "But after that story, I might be a happy landlubber for a while."

Jim leaned against the side of the convertible and said, "Whale watches are fascinating. I've gone on a few on the East Coast and hope to get one in when I'm in Washington later this year. They spot huge family groups of killer whales out there. You should go sometime. Seeing such huge creatures that live in an environment totally alien to how we live—it's incredible really. And you truly can't grasp the scale of a real whale until you've seen one breach right beside the rail where you're standing."

"Now you've sold me," Annie said. "You're going out West later this year?"

Jim nodded. "My publisher is already talking about the next lighthouse book. It'll be about Pacific Coast lighthouses. They have some great ghost stories out there too."

"Speaking of ghost stories," Alice interrupted, finally finding her keys. "We still have one more adventure to invite you on."

"Oh?" Annie paused before they climbed into the car. "What would that be?"

"A ghost walk!"

# ~ 14 ~

With Alice's words ringing in her head, Annie pushed the passenger seat forward as Jim opened the door. She slipped into the backseat and waited impatiently until her friends were in the car. "What kind of ghost walk are you talking about?"

"Alice is being dramatic," Jim said. "I actually want to get a feeling for what the lighthouse and the lighthouse road would be like at night in the rain. I can't walk the road," he said as he slapped his leg, "but Alice offered to do it and record her impressions. That way I can write about that part of the legend pretty accurately."

"Why don't you just use your memory of sneaking up there?" Annie asked. "That road is dangerous. I could see that when we walked it in broad daylight. Speaking as the mother of an ex-teenager, I would have grounded her for doing exactly what you're proposing."

"The difference," Alice said as she turned the key and coaxed the Mustang into a rumble, "is that we're not scared kids who can be spooked into running blindly in the rain, and I'm going to have one whopping big flashlight since I don't have to worry about hiding from the lighthouse keeper this time."

"*And* you want me to go with you?" Annie asked carefully.

Alice smiled at her in the rearview mirror. "I had hoped.

It would be more fun with both of us."

"When did you want to do this?" Annie asked as Alice eased the convertible out of the tiny parking lot and back onto the road. Though Alice didn't drive overly fast, the breeze immediately began to tangle Annie's hair, and she smoothed it down nervously.

"Tonight. The weather report is calling for rain, so it should reproduce the conditions perfectly for the curse. You and I will walk up the road and meet Jim at the top. I'm going to carry Jim's recorder so I can record our impressions as we walk along."

"I'll be taking photos of the lighthouse and the sea in the storm," Jim said. "It isn't supposed to be an electrical storm, and with the flashlights I bought today, you should have plenty of light to see. But if it worries you, don't feel like you have to come."

Annie hesitated. It sounded a lot like her dreams to her, and those were definitely not very comforting. At the same time, maybe it would be best to conquer her fear by facing it head-on. She glanced at Alice's hope-filled eyes in the mirror again and said, "OK, you can count me in."

Alice whooped and slapped her hand against the steering wheel. "That's great. Thanks so much."

"But that will mean I don't have time to go to the library today," Annie said. "I need to see if Gram left a proper New England raincoat in her closet. The coat I have is more for storms that aren't trying to pound you to death. It doesn't even have a hood, and I can't envision carrying an umbrella *and* a flashlight."

"The wind would make quick work of an umbrella," Jim

said. "Should we take you to buy a coat? I don't want you to be out there if you're not properly protected."

"I think I'll find something. Gram always embraced the idea of being prepared. I expect she has a coat that can handle any storm."

"Great," Alice said. "Should I take you home or back to Main Street? Did you park in town?"

"Yes," Annie said. "My car is near Mary Beth's shop. I think I still have time to pop in and volunteer to help if Mary Beth needs any help with the library crafts program.

"Oh great," Alice said. "Tell her to add my name too."

Alice pulled up beside Annie's burgundy Malibu, and Jim climbed out of the car to let Annie escape from the tight back seat. "Thanks again," Alice yelled as Jim slipped back into the car. "I'll come by Grey Gables tonight at about eight, and we'll get ready for the adventure!"

Annie nodded and smiled. Trust Alice to make a trudge through mud and rain sound like a thrill ride. She patted her trusty car on the hood as she walked by and headed to A Stitch in Time.

Mary Beth looked up as Annie walked through the door, her pixie smile as bright as the piles of yarn surrounding her on the counter. "Hey, Annie!" she exclaimed. "You came just in time to help me sort this new shipment." She held up a skein of cotton yarn. "Look at these colors!"

Annie looked over the new selection. She was drawn to a skein in a gorgeous mixture of rose, yellow, orange and chocolate brown, and when Annie turned the wrapper to find the color name, she found it was called "blushing sunset." Another wrapper declared itself "storm at sea" with a mix of grayish blues and greens. "Do you ever wonder who comes up with these color names?" she asked.

"Only when they don't make any sense at all," Mary Beth said. "I have one around here called 'Mother's Love.' How would anyone know what color that is?"

Annie shook her head. "What color is it?"

"A kind of creamy pink."

When they'd sorted most of the pile on the counter, Annie said, "I actually came in to pre-volunteer to help with the children's craft program at the library when it rolls around. I've been meaning to tell you, but I've been in a bit of a fog lately."

Mary Beth nodded. "I don't suppose you've learned who owned your lovely little rag doll?"

"Not exactly, but I think it was a friend of my mother's." Annie's face lit up as she told Mary Beth about finding her mother's journal. "I really feel like those few words I've read so far have opened a whole new window on my mother for me." Then Annie paused, nearly smacking herself in exasperation. "You know Liz Booth isn't that much older than my mother would be today. I should have asked her if she knew my mom when I talked to her today."

"You talked to Liz Booth?" Mary Beth said, surprise clear in her voice. The women of the Historical Society tended to be a bit like Stella, not exactly social chatterers. "Are you going to join the Historical Society?"

Annie shook her head. "I was with Alice and Jim Parker on a research mission for his book on the lighthouse. I guess I was so caught up in Liz's story about the old lighthouse keeper Matthew Murdoch that I didn't think about anything else. Did you know about him?"

"Some," Mary Beth said. "I met him once when I was in Magruder's to get groceries. I think it wasn't a long time before he died. As I remember, he stormed through the store, practically knocking people over. Then he was so grouchy with the cashier he made her cry."

"He'd been through a lot," Annie said, giving Mary Beth the condensed version of what Liz had told them.

"It never ceases to amaze me about all the different ways human beings deal with tragedy," the older woman said sadly. "Plus, I guess that's a reminder. You never know what someone might be going through."

Annie nodded. The bell above the door jingled, and Annie waited while Mary Beth turned her bright smile on a customer who had come in to buy an extra skein of yarn for a project. Annie let their voices wash over her while she gazed out the front windows. At some point, morning had turned to afternoon and shadows were lengthening. She realized she should be going soon, in case it took some time to find a proper raincoat.

The customer left smiling, and Annie told Mary Beth about her planned adventure with Alice.

"That doesn't sound terribly safe," Mary Beth said. "You be careful. That Alice can be entirely too brave for her own good sometimes."

Annie laughed aloud at that. "Actually Gram said those very words about Alice more than once."

She promised to be careful and to tell everything about the adventure at the next Hook and Needle meeting. "I expect most of the details will be soggy ones," she said. Then she excused herself and hurried out to the car. The drive back to Grey Gables was short, and Annie missed the breezy fun of Alice's convertible. If she ever traded in her beloved Malibu, maybe she would consider a wild choice like that for her next car. Then she chuckled. She'd certainly spend a lot more time straightening her hair if she did that.

When she pulled up in front of Grey Gables, the afternoon sun made the windows sparkle like gold. The bright wicker furniture on the wide front porch looked inviting, as if welcoming her back. Annie chuckled, thinking how much difference the sun could make.

She hopped out of the car and hurried inside. As always, Boots greeted her with a rundown of everything she'd missed while she was gone. At least, that's what Annie assumed the cat's long meowing monologues meant. It was possible they were just variations on "feed me" repeated over and over.

"I filled your bowl this morning," Annie said. "You should learn to pace yourself. I have a mission." Annie began poking through closets for a proper raincoat. She found one in a narrow closet off the back porch. The long green coat had a short attached cape across the back. Its heavy hood and oversized visor would help keep the rain off her face, while probably making her look like a big green duck. "Good thing it's not a fashion show," Annie said as she pulled out two matching rain boots. She tried everything on and found it would definitely suit her need.

Since the coat search took far less time than Annie

had expected, she decided to curl up with a sandwich and her mother's journal. She opened to the page where an old photo of her mother marked the spot.

*July 10th. The weather has turned hot and dry. I'm glad. Jo says we have to sneak up to the lighthouse at night in the rain, or it won't mean anything. She wants to show we're not afraid of the legend. I'm not afraid of the legend. Really, I'm not! But I don't like the idea of being out on that road on a rainy night, so every morning when the sun shines, I cheer.*

*July 15th. This weather is perfect for the beach. We go every day and swim. Jo got a new swimsuit, and it has two pieces!! Mom hasn't said anything, but I know she thinks it's scandalous. Everyone thinks it's scandalous. I could never ever wear that, but it looks perfect on Jo. Suddenly some of the boys on the beach want to hang out with us. They never did before. I know it's because of Jo's new suit.*

Annie stopped and rested her fingers lightly on the page, smiling. She was struck again by how much her mother's friendship reminded her of herself and Alice. She thought of the bikini Alice had bought with her birthday money one year. She'd kept it hidden from her mother for weeks. When her mother finally found it, she sewed a gingham skirt on the bottom of the bikini top and another on the bikini bottom. Alice had looked like a set of curtains! Annie laughed at the memory, making a mental note to tease Alice about it later.

*July 20th. Been so busy, it's hard to write. Yesterday, a boy bought me a shaved ice. I can't even write his name. It's just too embarrassing. He's got nice brown eyes. That's all I'm writing!*

*August 4th. He gave me a note!!!! I'm putting it in here. He doesn't come to the beach every day because he has to help his dad on the boat. I'm still not going to write his name, but I'll write his initials—CB. He's older than me, but I thought his poem was beautiful. Does he really think my hair looks like gold? I always think mine looks pale and dull next to Jo's.*

"Poor CB," Annie said, smiling at the tiny heart Judy had drawn beside the entry. CB may have been her mom's first crush, but ultimately he lost out to George Spencer.

*August 20th. School will be starting soon. It's still super dry here, and Mom's garden looks baked even though she waters it. I'm sorry for the farmers that Mom and Dad worry about, but all this dry weather has kept us on the beach and away from the lighthouse. CB bought me another shaved ice. Jo teases me constantly about him. I'm glad I didn't show her the poem. She would have laughed herself silly.*

*August 22nd. I just wish you couldn't see Butler's Light-house all the time in the distance. It keeps reminding Jo and Jenny. Please, just keep the sun shining.*

Annie flipped the page and tensed up. Her mother's handwriting was very different, almost sloppy. And all the little faces and doodles were gone from the page, replaced by smudges and water stains. She realized her mother must have been crying as she wrote the entry. Her hand trembled as she smoothed the page and began reading.

*September 10th. I haven't written because everything is so terrible now. We finally got rain on the night before school was going to start back. Jo was so excited. I suggested maybe just Jo and I should go, even though I was scared, but Jenny begged and begged.*

*It was horrible. I didn't know she would panic like that—we couldn't have known, could we? Now I wake up every morning hoping that that night was just a bad dream, but it was real. Horrible and real!!! Jo won't talk to me at all. Her mom glares at me if I come by the house. I even went back and found Matilda and took her to Jo's house last night. I had to throw pebbles at her window forever before she would come out. She screamed at me. She thinks it's my fault. I'm supposed to be the one who says when an idea is too much. I always stop in time. Always. Why didn't I?*

The writing became badly smudged after that and hard to read. Annie finally puzzled it out. Her mother was putting the doll and her journal in the attic to keep them safe until Jo wanted to be her friend again.

Tears collected in Annie's eyes as she stared at the last entry in her mother's journal. Apparently her mother's best friend had never forgiven her, since the doll had laid waiting in the attic for so many years. She couldn't imagine what she would have done if Alice had stopped being her friend when they were kids. They'd had their spats, but nothing that lasted.

"Poor Mom," Annie whispered.

She was so deeply into the past that she jumped and dropped her mother's journal on the floor when she heard a knock on the front door. She wiped her eyes and took a few deep breaths before hurrying through the house to answer it.

As she neared the front screen door, she recognized the three grinning faces of Wally, Peggy, and Emily. Peggy wore her pink waitress uniform, so Annie assumed she was dashing over on her supper break. Wally was turned sideways and appeared to be trying to hide something behind Peggy's back while Emily giggled.

Annie opened the screen and gasped as Wally turned and held up a wooden lobster boat on wheels. "Oh, my," she said. "It's wonderful. Please, come in!"

Emily dashed in first, jumping up and down beside Annie. Annie smiled down at her. It was clear Emily was completely healed from the broken leg she'd gotten at the end of last summer. "I helped make it," the six-year-old said. "I ate a whole box of Popsicles so Daddy could use the sticks!" The little girl wore a pink T-shirt with a group of princesses on the front. Most of her pink shorts were covered by a fluffy pink tutu. Her long dark hair was done up in a single braid that jumped when she did.

"Wow," Annie said. "That must have been yummy."

"It was," Emily answered as she pointed to a lobster pot on the deck of the boat. "See, those are some of the sticks. Daddy made them look old." Then she pointed at the wheelhouse on the deck of the ship. "See that wheel? It really turns. I turned it!"

"Emily was a big help," Wally said, resting his hand on the little girl's shoulder.

"This is totally amazing, Wally," Annie said as she looked closely at all the tiny details. A tiny rope lay coiled up on the deck of the boat, and painted lobster floats hung on more tiny ropes off the side. The small wheelhouse had a door that opened on hinges, and another trapdoor opened a large part of the deck so John could play with the space below, where Wally had built a small cabin. "It's absolutely beautiful. When I take this to Texas, all the little boys John knows are going to want one. Shall I take orders?"

"Well, I don't mind doing more of these," Wally said. "It was fun."

"He's making mine first," Emily said seriously. "It's going to be pink and purple, and it's going to be for catching mermaids, not icky lobsters."

"I think that sounds like a totally perfect boat!" Annie said.

Annie glanced at Peggy and noticed the young woman watching her closely with her warm brown eyes. "Are you all right, Annie?" she asked. Then she leaned closer and whispered, "You look like you've been crying."

Annie squeezed Peggy's hand warmly. "I was reading an old diary of my mother's when she was a girl. It had some sad parts, but you all have certainly cheered me up with this wonderful boat."

"Well, it's a little rough in spots," Wally said modestly, though his face glowed at Annie's praise.

"Daddy's going have a boat just like this someday, only big," Emily said. "He's going to name it after me!"

"Sounds perfect," Annie said. "Now, let me get my checkbook so I can pay you. This is absolutely amazing!" Annie retrieved her purse and asked Wally what he wanted for the boat. The amount he quoted was so low that Annie simply wrote the check for what she felt the boat was worth. She tore it off and handed it to him. "There, that's what I insist on paying and no argument!"

Wally's eyes opened wide. "Wow, you certainly don't haggle like a New Englander!"

"If anyone in Texas wants one, I'm going to ask for

even more," Annie said. "I consider this the special price for close friends."

Peggy laughed. "Well, don't price it so high that no one wants one."

Annie ran her hand over the bow of the ship. "I don't think you have to worry about that. This is going to make my grandson so happy. Now, can I get you all any refreshments? I have some iced tea and might be able to scare up some cookies."

Emily's face lit up, but Peggy glanced at her watch and yelped. "I'm sorry, we have to run," she called as she caught hold of Emily's hand. "We'll talk more at the Hook and Needle Club meeting."

"OK. Thanks again, Wally," Annie said.

Emily pulled loose of her mother's hand and gave Annie a quick hug before dashing outside and skipping across the porch. Wally and Peggy followed, and Annie smiled as she saw Peggy slip her hand into Wally's as they walked.

# ~ 15 ~

As Annie watched the Carson family leave, her stomach growled. She had been so busy all day that she hadn't really eaten unless she counted a muffin, eggs and toast, and the sandwich that lay mostly uneaten on the plate. She'd gotten so caught up in her mother's journal that she'd forgotten about eating.

She poked the sandwich and decided the bread seemed soft enough. She'd add a cup of soup and call it supper. If she didn't let herself get distracted by anything else, she should be able to eat before Alice arrived.

As Anne stood at the stove, warming a thick vegetable soup she'd made during the frosty winter and frozen, Boots appeared magically as she always did whenever someone might accidentally drop some food on the floor. "Don't think I didn't notice you made yourself scarce when Emily was here," she told the cat. "She's a very nice little girl."

Boots meowed skeptically, and Annie shook her head with a smile. Wayne had never been fond of animals, so Annie hadn't been a pet owner for years, but she was beginning to understand the attraction. Boots must have been great company for Gram, and Annie was glad to have her around—even if the cat did project an air of superiority much of the time.

"I'll just pretend I'm living with a teenager," Annie said

as she poured the hot soup into a mug and carried it to the table.

As she sipped the soup, Annie wondered how much of her dreams were accurate. She was almost certain now that they must have come from something she'd been told as a child and then forgotten. No doubt the details now were being expanded every time she learned something new. Her mother's journal had not been specific about exactly what had happened, but her journal fit so perfectly with what Annie remembered of her dreams that she was left with a deep sense of foreboding about little Jenny.

Shaking off such gloomy thoughts, Annie finally rinsed her mug and plate. Her timing was just about perfect. She heard knocking as she shut off the water, and found Alice standing on the front porch. A long, black raincoat hung nearly to the middle of her shins and the hood covered almost all of her face. She carried a huge flashlight in each hand.

"Where did you get that coat?" Annie asked as she pulled the door open.

Alice pushed the hood back and followed Annie into the house. "When Jim and I stopped by the hardware store today, I told Mike Malone that I needed a serious raincoat, and it turned out that he had this one."

"It definitely looks serious," Annie agreed. "You look like the grim reaper."

Alice laughed. "I'll have to keep it around for Halloween then. Maybe Mike can fix me up with a scythe to go with it."

"As long as you don't carry it tonight," Annie said. "I'm nervous enough."

"No reason to be." Alice handed Annie one of the heavy flashlights. "You could light up a runway with these things. Plus, it's not even raining yet. I think it's going to later; you should wear a raincoat too. Did you find one?"

Annie nodded as they walked through the kitchen and into the back mudroom. She picked up the heavy green coat. "It's just about as stylish as yours."

"Adventuring is rough business."

Annie shrugged into the coat and stuffed the wooden toggles through the thick loops that held together the front of the coat. She was happy to miss out on the rain, but she hoped the walk would be cool. The heavy coat would get hot fast if it wasn't.

She led the way back through the house. When they passed through the kitchen, Boots raised her head from the bowl of cat crunchies. One wide-eyed look at the women in their flappy coats was enough for the cat, and she dashed under the kitchen table to hide until they passed.

"Everyone's a fashion critic," Alice said, giggling.

Annie flipped on the front porch light to help them see their way across the yard. The stretch of Ocean Drive in front of Grey Gables didn't have a streetlight. Annie was still getting used to how dark night seemed to be in New England, and how quickly night fell. The time from sunset to pitch dark was almost like flipping a switch on cloudy nights like this one. Back in Texas, she and Wayne sometimes sat on the porch for hours after sunset since the streetlights chased the shadows from their yard.

After they left the comforting pool of porch light, they would need to rely on the flashlights, or risk tripping and falling before the adventure even got started. It might not be raining yet, but the thick cloud cover blocked out any light the full moon might offer.

As they clattered down the porch steps, the wind tossed Annie's fine hair into her face. She shuddered as she noticed the beautiful weeping willow near the corner of the yard looming at them like a sea monster, massive arms dripping with seaweed. Annie shook her head ruefully. She had entirely too much imagination sometimes. To distract herself, she said, "I finished my mother's journal today."

Alice jumped at the sound of Annie's voice. "Really?" she said, her voice distracted. "Did you find out who owned the doll?"

"A little girl named Jenny." Annie sighed, realizing this wasn't going to be a good distraction for a spooky night. "Mom never mentioned any last names. I'm not even sure how old the girls were because Mom didn't put year dates on her entries. Something bad happened to the little girl though, and it drove a wedge between Mom and her best friend."

Alice looked toward Annie, her face moon-pale in the black night. "That's sad," she said. "I can sort of relate to that. I missed you when you stopped coming back to Stony Point. It's been great reconnecting."

"It's meant a lot to me too," Annie said.

They fell silent as they paused at the empty road to turn on their flashlights, each caught up in her own thoughts. "Mom couldn't have been a little girl in the journal, since she was old enough for her first crush," Alice said, remembering the cheerier things she had read. "I found out the young man who sent her the love poem had the initials CB.

Mom was too embarrassed to even write out his name."

"Your mother sounds like you," Alice said as they hurried across the road. "Shy about her love life."

Annie noticed the chain was still piled on the pillar that marked the beginning of the lighthouse road. That made sense if Jim had driven up to the lighthouse earlier. Annie shone her light on the small sign that seemed to be warning her away from this particular adventure. "The sign says we shouldn't go up there," she said.

"That makes it more fun." Alice saluted the little sign as she started up the gravel road.

Annie peeked sideways at her friend. "You know, if I ever start having a love life, I promise to tell you about it. And that reminds me. How's your love life?"

"Subtle," Alice said. "Very subtle. Jim and I are doing fine. He's a nice guy."

"A nice guy who is only staying in Stony Point a little longer before heading to the West Coast," Annie reminded her.

"You caught that, huh?" Alice said. She stopped for a moment and looked up. "I think I just felt a raindrop."

"You're just stalling," Annie said accusingly. Then she felt a fat raindrop plop on her nose. "OK, I take that back. It's raining."

Both women pulled the hoods over their heads. Rain pattered against the thick rubber of the hood, making Annie feel secluded in the thick hood. She swept the ground ahead of her with the bright flashlight beam.

They reached the beginning of the stand of trees that edged the road as it began the climb to the lighthouse. Annie played her flashlight over the twisted branches of the trees.

Foliage always seemed scant on these trees, as if the constant wind from the sea blew the leaves away. The moving light made shadows dance as if something flitted through the trees just beyond the light. Annie knew it was an illusion, but it was unnerving just the same.

"Jim asked me to go with him," Alice almost whispered.

Alice's voice coming out of the darkness behind her startled Annie so badly she nearly dropped her flashlight. Then she processed Alice's actual *words*. "Jim asked you to go with him when he leaves? Are you considering it?"

"He's gorgeous," Alice said, and Annie heard the thick rubber of Alice's coat rustle as she shrugged. "He makes me laugh. He knows the most incredible stories. I don't think that life could ever be dull around Jim."

"So you're going?" Annie's voice crept up an octave. She couldn't imagine Stony Point without Alice. The ease with which they'd reconnected when Annie came back to Grey Gables had made the years melt away. She had other friends, but only Alice really felt like family.

Alice's dark hood turned toward her, her face invisible in the shadow, and Annie was struck again by how much the black raincoat made her look like the grim reaper. But Alice's voice was as warm and lively as ever. "I haven't made my decision, but I definitely will admit I'm tempted."

They fell silent again, trudging through the dark and rain. The wind picked up, blowing rain in on Annie's face now. The steady drumming on the hood of her coat felt more like pounding. Had her mother really come out here without a raincoat? In her dream, Judy and the other girls always wore summery dresses. Annie couldn't imagine struggling through this kind of weather in the pitch dark with no protection at all from the sting of the wind-driven rain.

The incline of the road sharpened, and Annie felt it in every step as her calves threatened to cramp. *I really need to get more exercise*, she thought. The wind howled up from the cliff side of the road, and the mournful sound made the legend's talk of lost souls all the more chilling. She could almost imagine voices calling out in the wind.

"*Annie!*" it howled, and Annie grabbed Alice's arm, the sleeve of her coat slick under her hand.

"Did you hear that?" she asked.

"What?"

"Someone calling my name!"

Alice's dark hood shook. "It's the wind—and your imagination."

Annie shook her head. It was *not* her imagination. Alice's deeper, thicker hood, and maybe her preoccupation with Jim, must have kept her from hearing it. Annie turned and backtracked a few steps so the sounds could funnel into her hood more clearly.

"Annie!" the wind howled louder. "Alice!"

"You had to hear that!" she said.

This time Alice turned around also. The two women turned their flashlights to the road behind them. Who could be coming up behind them on a night like this? Jim would be in front of them, not behind.

"Annie! Alice!" The voice was unmistakably male. The women began walking back down the road slowly, their flashlights searching the darkness. Rain drove against their backs now, pushing them hard and making Annie stumble as the loose gravel shifted under her feet. She remembered her dream of the little girl's feet slipping along the road as she tried to run home to safety. Annie played her flashlight off to either side to be certain she was safely centered on the narrow road. With the shoving of the wind, it would be so easy to wander to one side or the other.

"Annie!" The voice was much stronger now. Annie felt a nudge of familiarity, but she couldn't place it. Who was it? What did he want with them?

Finally their flashlight beams met the edge of another light beam that seemed to be climbing the steep road toward them. Annie struggled to see beyond the source of the light, but all she could see was a tall dark shadow against the still darker night.

"I'm glad I found you!" the figure shouted, and finally Annie recognized it.

"Ian!" she said, her knees weak with relief as she played her flashlight over his tall figure. He wore a heavy orange all-weather coat that hung just past his waist but had no hood. Instead Anne could see a small slice of the watch cap showing under the hood of a fleece jacket that Ian wore under the raincoat. Annie suspected the hat and hoodie wouldn't cause the tunnel vision of her deep hood and wished she had something like that.

She also realized the rain had slacked off again at just about the exact moment the mayor showed up. The wind no longer seemed to be trying to push her off her feet. She pushed the hood back on her head. The rain felt more like mist on her face, and she sighed with relief. "What are you doing out here, Ian?"

The mayor covered the rest of the ground between them quickly with his long-legged stride, his heavy boots splashing puddles as he walked. "Mary Beth told me about your planned 'adventure.' I was shocked to hear you'd take a crazy risk like this. This road is dangerous in the daytime, so I certainly wasn't going to leave you out here in the dark alone."

"*Hello!*" Alice said, following Annie's lead to push back her own hood. "She's not alone! I'm here."

"I meant that as a plural 'you,'" he said.

Alice muttered, "Sure you did."

Ian turned his bewildered gaze toward Alice. "Consider me an official escort for *both* of you."

"Well, I'm glad to have you along," Annie said as the three of them began trudging up the hill again.

"Exactly why are you battling a storm on a road bordered by a cliff?" Ian asked.

"We're collecting atmosphere," Alice said.

"Atmosphere?"

"For Jim Parker's book," she explained. "That way he can include firsthand details about what this creepy walk is like."

"Why isn't Mr. Parker here collecting his own details instead of sending you out here?" Ian asked, his voice heavy with disapproval. "He should at least walk along with you."

"Jim walks with two prosthetic legs," Alice said her voice rising slightly with anger. "I suspect this road would be considerably more dangerous for him than for two perfectly capable women. And he didn't *send* me, I volunteered."

"Please don't fight," Annie implored. She then paused,

feeling a rush of déjà vu at her words. "This weather is miserable enough. We're doing a favor for a friend who couldn't do it for himself."

Ian didn't respond for a moment. "I'm sorry," he said finally. "I didn't know about Mr. Parker's condition. I was worried about both of you."

"You certainly take the job of protecting your constituency very seriously," Alice said dryly. "And it *was* creepy out here."

"I especially noticed the trees when we started out," Annie said. "You should mention that to Jim. The wind on this peninsula has twisted the trees until they look very menacing in the flashlight beam." Annie found talking about the details made them seem a little less scary. Then she stopped and stared at her friend. "I thought you were supposed to be using a recorder to keep track of these spooky details."

"I was, but ... " Alice paused and grinned sheepishly as she pulled a small recorder from her pocket, " ... I forgot to buy batteries for it. Those things eat up batteries really fast. Besides, I can remember all the details. Scary trees, scary howling wind, scary mayor sneaking up behind you," Alice said, ticking the items off on her fingers.

Ian reached over and folded down one finger. "Not sneaking. I yelled for you the whole time."

"That's true," Annie said. "Alice suggested I was imagining things when I heard the wind call my name."

"Sorry about that," Alice said.

"Well, I did imagine the weeping willow in my yard looked like a swamp monster," Annie said. "So you probably weren't being totally unfair."

"Swamp monster?" Ian said, laughing.

Annie gave him a playful shove. "You should look at one in the dark sometime."

"After you planted the swamp monster image?" Ian said. "I'll never go near one again."

"Our brave hero," Alice said, and Annie was glad to hear her friend's normal warm teasing tone.

The rain picked up again, and both women hurried to pull their hoods back over their heads before they were drenched. They walked in silence for a while, saving their breath for the steep road. Then suddenly, lightning split the sky, and Annie saw the hulking outline of buildings and knew they were almost to the top of the road.

"I thought it wasn't supposed to be an electrical storm," she shouted to Alice.

"Blame the weatherman," Alice shouted back. "At least we made it."

They reached the small parking lot at the end of the road. Annie played her light over the raised flower bed and stone benches that had been so charming in the daylight. Now they mostly offered obstacles to fall over.

"Jim!" Alice bellowed, but the howling wind blew the words back into her face.

If Jim answered, it must have been snatched away by the gale that whistled through the buildings. They swept their flashlight beams over the parking lot and the strip of grassy lawn beside it, looking for any sign of him. They spotted his rental car at the edge of the parking lot. "He's here somewhere," Alice said, turning her flashlight toward the hulking buildings.

"We'll find him," Annie said.

"Maybe we should split up?" Ian suggested reluctantly. "We could find him quicker that way. If this is turning into an electrical storm, I don't think we should be out in it any longer than we have to."

The women nodded and each picked their direction after a brief discussion. Ian headed toward the cliff's edge in case Jim was shooting photos of the rocky shore in the storm. Alice headed in toward the lighthouse keeper's cottage, in case Jim had finished shooting and was taking shelter. And Annie headed toward the lighthouse itself.

She'd walked barely a few steps from her friends before she felt totally alone. The sound of the rain on her hood drowned out every other noise. And her flashlight beam struggled to push back the darkness worsened by the driving rain.

As she walked, she imagined again the terrifying experience her mother must have had up here with her friends, especially when Jenny ran away from the others. It would be impossible to find anyone in the crushing darkness. Finally, Annie's flashlight beam swept across the stone blocks of the lighthouse.

She turned and began circling the lighthouse, keeping the wall on her right side so that she didn't lose track of it and wander off. "Jim!" she shouted over and over until her throat felt dry and rough. She paused after each call to listen for a response, but with the drumming rain, Jim could be yelling to her from a few yards away, and she would never hear him.

She stepped closer to the lighthouse and rested her hand on the rough, wet rock. That's what Annie's mother and her friends had come up here to do. They just wanted to touch the lighthouse and prove they were brave. A simple thing, and it may have killed little Jenny.

Annie's fingers probed the crevices of the rock. Had Jenny really died in whatever accident her mother's journal hinted at? Annie didn't know for sure. Certainly something bad had happened, but her mother didn't say Jenny had died. It seemed likely, but she could have gotten badly hurt. Jenny's big sister might have felt just as angry about a terrible injury. Annie decided that tomorrow she was definitely going to find out what happened and who Jenny was.

The pounding rain on Annie's hood stopped so suddenly that she wondered for a split second if she'd simply gone deaf. The rain was taking another break. Annie picked up her pace, eager to finish the circle of the lighthouse and find someone so she wasn't alone in the dark anymore.

The ground under her feet felt like sodden sponge, splashing with each step, and then clinging to her boot a moment before letting go with a wet sucking sound. The wet slurping reminded Annie again of monsters, and she missed the rain drowning out the other sounds. She shook her head ruefully. She was entirely too old to entertain quite so much imagination.

Then she heard a giggle. Just up ahead someone had laughed. Someone young. Annie froze. Was her imagination working overtime again?

# — 16 —

Annie shielded the beam of her flashlight with her hand, and then slowed down and crept forward, following the lighthouse wall. She heard another giggle and the definite sound of voices. If she was having some kind of hallucination, it certainly was persistent.

As she rounded the curve, she spotted two teenage girls in sodden jeans and muddy sneakers. Each wore a dark hoodie that turned their faces into round pale circles as she turned the flashlight toward them. Both girls screamed. Annie recognized one of the round-eyed faces immediately. "Vanessa?" she said.

"Mrs. Dawson?" Kate's daughter shielded her eyes and tried to see past the flashlight. Annie lowered the beam and walked closer to the girls.

"Busted!" the second girl said in a loud whisper.

"I recognize you too, Mackenzie," Annie said. Vanessa and Mackenzie went to high school together and had become good friends during a teen needlework project the Hook and Needle Club had gotten involved in a month before. Clearly their interests had taken a turn toward ghost stories. In their matching sodden outfits with their long brown hair stuffed into hoodies, they looked like sisters.

"We weren't doing anything wrong," Mackenzie protested. "We just wanted to touch the lighthouse, and then we were going straight home. I swear."

"So did you touch it?" Annie asked. "Because we're definitely going to do the 'straight home' part."

"Not yet," Vanessa said sheepishly. "We were working up to it. We thought we might have seen a ghost … maybe. And we ran and got a little lost next to the buildings. Then we only just found the lighthouse when your flashlight almost gave us heart attacks."

"It's just a lighthouse, girls," Annie said, reaching out and resting her hand on the rough stones again. "There's no ghost or curse. It's just a lighthouse on a dangerous road that you should not be walking on in a storm."

"Oh?" Mackenzie said with a grin. "How did you get up here?"

Annie decided not to get into a discussion of her own poor decisions. "Have you two seen anyone else up here? An older man who walks with a limp?"

"Yeah," Vanessa said, breathlessly. She glanced nervously back the way of the other buildings. "He was tromping around the porch to the lighthouse keeper's cottage. You mean he's a real person?"

"Of course he's real," Mackenzie said as she rolled her eyes. "There's no such thing as ghosts."

"Don't pretend you weren't scared," Vanessa said, putting her hands on her hips. "You thought he might be the lighthouse keeper's ghost too. I wasn't the only one running."

Annie suppressed a laugh. She looked forward to telling Jim Parker that he'd been mistaken for a ghost. "OK, touch the lighthouse quickly, and I'll take you to meet the lighthouse keeper's ghost. Maybe I can borrow his car and take you both home."

"Oh, you don't have to do that, Mrs. Dawson," Vanessa said earnestly. "We don't mind walking."

"*I* mind," Annie said. "That road is dangerous enough going *up*. Let's go."

The two girls slapped hands against the side of the lighthouse and then tromped along beside Annie. "Do you have to tell my mom?" Vanessa asked. "She's going to freak. She can be way overprotective sometimes."

"Mine too," Mackenzie muttered. "I'll be grounded until I'm old and feeble."

"I'll think about it," Annie said, weakening slightly. After all, her reason for walking to the lighthouse in a storm might have been more sensible, but it was still probably not a good idea. She certainly understood the lure of adventure, especially as a teenager. Her grandparents used to blame their graying hair on the stunts she and Alice pulled as teens.

They walked without speaking; the only sounds were the squish of each step on the sodden ground. Then Annie heard more splashing and sloshing, only coming ahead of them. She smiled and picked up her pace, ready to rejoin her friends. The light of her flashlight met the glow coming around the side of the lighthouse, and she heard the mayor's deep smooth voice. "Annie?"

"I'm here," she said, "and I've made a discovery!"

The girls giggled at that, and Annie heard a questioning sound from Ian. Then they rounded the last bit of curve, and she could see the dark outline of her friend. "Vanessa and Mackenzie decided to brave the curse," Annie said. "They said they saw Jim at the lighthouse keeper's cottage. Is he still there?"

"He is," Ian said. "Alice is with him. I came to track you down."

"I thought I would ask to borrow his rental car and drive these ladies home," Annie said.

"That sounds like a job for the mayor," Ian said. "We can have a talk about keeping my constituents safe. But you can definitely ride along too." He added the last part with a grin, his white teeth flashing in the dim light.

"Um, Mr. Mayor," Mackenzie said. "If we promise to never do anything like this again … "

"*Ever!*" Vanessa added vehemently.

" … could you not tell on us?" Mackenzie finished.

"That doesn't sound very fair to your parents," Ian said. "I expect they would want to know about this."

Both girls drooped like wilted roses, and Annie felt like a jailor leading two condemned prisoners as they trudged the rest of the way to the cottage. She was delighted to see the porch was now lit. The cozy glow warmed the night and helped chase away the last of the creepiness from the experience.

She spotted Alice and Jim leaning against the porch rail with their heads together peering at the preview screen on the back of his camera. Jim looked up at the approaching group, and Annie saw him nudge Alice.

"Looks like you picked up some extra adventurers," Alice called. "Who are your soggy new friends?"

"Oh, you'll recognize this pair," Annie said. The girls looked up then, and waved weakly.

"Vanessa! Mackenzie! Hi," Alice said. "Did you see any ghosts?"

"Only him," Mackenzie said, nodding at Jim.

Jim laughed. "I'm not dead yet, young lady."

"This is Jim Parker," Alice said. "He's researching the lighthouse and the legend. So, did you two touch the lighthouse?"

The girls nodded. Then Vanessa said, "Mrs. Dawson touched it first."

Alice and Jim raised their eyebrows and looked at Annie at the same moment, which made her laugh. "I was just showing them that nothing would happen," she said.

Ian spoke up, his voice a bit strained. "I was hoping we could borrow your car and take these girls home."

"That's probably a good idea," Jim said. He seemed totally oblivious to the mayor's sudden change in mood. "We definitely won't all fit in the car. While you're gone, I can retake a few shots that didn't come out like I'd like. I should be done by the time you get back."

"I'll stay here with Jim," Alice added.

"Fine," Ian said.

Annie looked up at him curiously, noticing the strain in his jaw. She turned to Jim and said, "Thanks."

"No problem," Jim said.

But Annie could plainly see there was a problem. Had something happened while she was splashing around in the dark? Ian herded the girls toward the small lighthouse parking lot, and they climbed into Jim's rental car. Annie saw he'd thrown towels over the seats, but she suspected they wouldn't help much with the water dripping from all of them.

Ian left his door open while he swept the hood from his head and pulled off the wet watch cap. He wrung it out over the gravel of the parking lot before laying it on the floor at Annie's feet. She smiled at Ian's hat hair. Small tufts of salt and pepper stood up in spots, giving him a rakish look. She considered mentioning it, but the stiffness in Ian's jaw made her nervous. What was wrong?

Annie sat quietly while Ian drove down the steep road, though the two girls whispered and occasionally giggled in the backseat. As they bumped gently out onto Ocean Drive, Ian finally spoke, "Now that I've walked up the lighthouse road in the rain, I know exactly how foolish it is. You risked getting seriously hurt or killed."

"We were really careful," Vanessa said earnestly.

"And we had flashlights," Mackenzie added.

"And you had a storm and loose gravel and the potential for being struck by lightning," Ian said. "What would have happened if the flashlights had gone out, and you had wandered off the side of the road?"

The girls didn't answer and the silence in the car stretched. Finally Vanessa spoke in a near whisper. "We won't do it again."

"I hope not," Ian said, glancing sternly at them in the rearview mirror. "I'm glad you didn't pay too high a price for doing it this time."

"Um," Mackenzie said, "just how high is the price going to be this time? I mean, are you going to tell on us?"

Ian sighed. "You're not children, so here's what I'm going to do. If you will both volunteer to help with at least three community projects this summer, *and* if I don't hear of any more bad decisions by the two of you, this can stay between us. You can start with helping out at the library.

Valerie Duffy was in my office just last week looking for ideas to increase teen participation. It looks like you ladies will be providing a little boost."

"Yes, sir," Vanessa said eagerly. "We can do that."

"Totally," Mackenzie agreed.

"And if I catch you two doing anything else foolish, all bets are off," Ian said. "I'll include this incident when I haul you in front of your parents for the next one."

"You won't catch us again," Mackenzie promised.

Watching the girls in her visor mirror, Annie saw Vanessa nudge Mackenzie hard and give her a look. "Because we won't do anything else stupid," Vanessa said. "I promise." Mackenzie grinned back and shrugged.

"OK. Don't make me sorry I agreed to it," Ian said. "I expect to see the list of projects you're going to take part in by the end of the week. You can drop it by my office."

"Yes, sir," the girls said together, clearly relieved.

The rest of the ride to their houses passed quickly. Ian waited at the curb until each of the girls was safely inside. Then he turned around to head back toward the lighthouse. "Do you want me to drop you at Grey Gables?" he asked.

"Actually, I'd like you to tell me what you're so angry about," Annie said.

Ian didn't answer for a moment as he stared straight ahead into the night. Finally, he blew out a frustrated breath. "I don't like Jim Parker talking you and Alice into something as foolish as walking that road in the rain," he said. "It was irresponsible."

"Alice and I are grown women," Annie said. "We made our own decisions."

"Then why were you on a loose gravel road in the pitch dark chasing some ridiculous legend like a kid?" he asked, his voice raising slightly.

"We weren't chasing a legend," Annie said. "We were doing research."

"Research?" Ian snapped. "That's the most stupid excuse I've ever … " Then he stopped.

"Stupid?" Annie said, her voice very quiet. "Did you just call me stupid?"

"No," Ian said. "I was just worried."

"Worried about how stupid I am?" Annie said, her voice still deadly calm and quiet. She knew the decision to walk up the gravel road wasn't the smartest she'd made since coming back to Stony Point, but hearing the word "stupid" directed at her made her swell with anger.

"I should not have said stupid. But when I got that call from Mary Beth, I was worried. I don't want anything to happen to you. I *like* you, Annie Dawson. I like you a *lot*." He paused at Annie's sharp intake of breath and raised one hand to hold off her comment. "I know we're just friends. I'm fine with being friends. It's good, and I'm not trying to step over any lines here. But if I see you in danger, I'm not going to sit back and say nothing."

All of Annie's righteous indignation at being called stupid drained away in a wave of confusion. She wasn't sure exactly what Ian was confessing about his feelings, but she knew it was something she wasn't ready to deal with. "I'm sorry I worried you," she said softly. "But you have no reason to be mad at Jim. He didn't make anyone do anything. I'm pretty sure this was Alice's idea—not Jim's."

Ian didn't answer for a moment; then he nodded, his eyes firmly on the road ahead. "He still went along with it. He seems to care about Alice. That's what confuses me. How could he let her do something so … "

"Stupid?" Annie asked.

"Dangerous."

"I suspect Jim is an adventurer. He doesn't think about danger like you do, or even like I do. And I think maybe there's a little of that in Alice too." She sighed. "But that road scared me half to death, and I was very glad when you showed up. I don't think I'm much of an adventurer."

Ian turned to smile at her, and then brought his eyes back to the road with a laugh. "Your track record since you came back to Stony Point sure makes you look adventurous."

"I don't know how I get into these things," Annie said, shaking her head. "I'm really a big chicken at heart."

"But a curious chicken," Ian said, still chuckling, "with a stubborn streak a mile wide." He turned onto Ocean Drive and asked. "So Grey Gables or back to the lighthouse?"

"I'd like to go to Grey Gables," she said. "I'm suddenly really tired of being cold and wet. I think Alice probably soaked up enough atmosphere on the road for both of us. Please, tell them I'm going to finish the library research tomorrow. If you don't think that will be too dangerous, Mr. Mayor?"

"It sounds safe enough," Ian said, "but I'm starting to realize you can find trouble anywhere."

"Oh, I hope not," Annie said, though she was starting to suspect Ian might be right.

# ~ 17 ~

*T*he driving rain struck the young blond girl's arms like thrown stones. She lagged behind her tall friend as if pulled from behind. The gap between them grew wider.

"Come on, Judy," Jo yelled as she raised an arm to shield her eyes from the rain. "As soon as we touch the lighthouse we can go home."

"I'm worried about Jenny," Judy shouted. "I should go back."

"She'll be fine. It's not like there are wolves in the woods." Jo tromped back down the road and tugged on Judy's arm. "Let's go. The sooner we do it, the sooner we can be home. We're going to be in trouble when we get home. I just want to make sure it's worth it."

Judy looked into the darkness behind her. She started to turn away when both girls heard a scream.

"Jenny!" Judy's shout was raw and thin. She scrambled down the gravel road, the loose rocks sliding under the slick soles of her shoes. Jo passed her on the road, thundering down into the darkness, screaming her sister's name.

Annie woke with a start, almost surprised to find sunshine pouring through her windows. She remembered more of the dream this time, and the feeling in her dream of her mother's panic left her shaken. Something terrible had happened on that steep, stormy road, and Annie vowed not to let one more day pass before she found out exactly what it was.

As she dressed for the day in crisp cotton pants and a soft aqua tee, Annie realized she was beginning to treat the dreams like some kind of revelation. She'd never believed that dreams were more than movies from your imagination, but these dreams certainly seemed to be showing her something that really happened.

After a quick breakfast, Annie drove into town. This time she parked as close to the library as possible. She didn't want to risk running into anyone who might distract her from her goal.

The rain had left the air fresh, and the sky was a dazzling blue with only a few cottony puffs. A light breeze cooled Annie's face as she closed the car door. It was a perfect Stony Point day with no sign of the storm that had made the night so frightening.

"Annie!"

"Oh no!" Annie whispered. *I'm going to the library*, she reminded herself as she turned around to face whomever had called out her name. It was Kate, waving from the sidewalk in front of The Cup & Saucer.

"Hold on just a second," Kate said. The breeze stirred her dark hair as she hurried across the street. When she reached Annie, she gave her a quick hug, turning her warm smile up to full wattage. "I wanted to thank you for getting Vanessa safely home!"

"Oh, she told you?" Annie said.

"I caught her dripping all the way to her room," Kate said. "Vanessa never could lie, thank goodness. She told me about her adventure with Mackenzie at the lighthouse. And that you and Ian drove her home. Since she looked like she'd been in-volved in a near drowning, braving the lighthouse curse seemed a lot less terrible than my first guess."

"Ian will be disappointed that she's off the hook," Annie said. "He was hoping to get some community service out of her and Mackenzie."

"Oh, he still will. It was that or grounding," Kate said. "Besides, I couldn't be too mad at her … " she looked both ways mysteriously and then whispered. " … Harry and I snuck up there when we were teenagers. I was scared to death, but I think Harry liked the chance to be my brave hero. I'd feel like a hypocrite if I were too harsh. Though when I think about Van-essa being out on that narrow road in a storm … Anyway—I'm grateful to you and Ian for getting her home safely. Now, what were you doing up there in the middle of the night?"

"Research for Jim Parker's book on the lighthouse," Annie said, "and probably proving Alice and I still haven't grown up."

Kate laughed. "I think we should never have to grow up too much. Well, I need to dash. Mary Beth will be wondering where I am. Thanks again."

"No problem," Annie said. "I'm glad to have helped." She watched her friend dash back across the road and hurry up the sidewalk. For a moment, Annie just enjoyed the thought of how many friends she'd made in less than a year at Stony Point. Then she turned and crossed the sidewalk to the steps of the library.

As always, she paused to look at the beautiful building. A brass plaque next to the door declared it had been built as a private home in the 1840s. Back home in Texas, it was rare to see truly old buildings. But in New England, many homes bore little plaques that gave the year they were built and listed who the first owners had been. Annie liked that feeling of living and walking through history every day.

She strolled up the steps and ran a hand over one of the tall white columns. The feeling was so different from the rough lighthouse rock. History had texture, Annie knew. Some of it was bright and smooth, and some dark and rough. The history she was looking for today couldn't help but be rough.

Annie sighed and pushed open the multipaned glass door. Her sandals tapped lightly on the wood floor as she crossed the foyer, throwing a quick nod to the portrait of the library volunteer of the year.

Sun streamed through the tall windows in the Great Room, welcoming Annie to one of her favorite places. Then, she stopped for a moment and blinked. The library volunteer of the year—Josephine Booth—stood behind the circulation desk, sorting through a pile of books. Annie smiled. She was finally going to meet the mysterious Ms. Booth. She picked up her pace and headed straight for the desk; her research could wait a few minutes.

The tall, older woman looked up at Annie as she approached and smiled slightly. Annie was struck by the sense of quiet surrounding the woman, as if she tried not to disturb the air around her too much. The woman's hair was snowy white and styled in delicate waves away from her face.

"Hello," Annie said. "I'm Annie Dawson, and you're Josephine Booth." The older woman raised her eyebrows in mild surprise, and Annie added, "I've seen your volunteer picture so many times, I just had to introduce myself."

Ms. Booth nodded. "Annie Dawson. I've heard about you from Valerie and Grace. You're always tracking down information about things from Grey Gables."

"It does feel like that sometimes," Annie said. "Though today I'm on a mission for a friend, but I had to introduce myself first."

Ms. Booth nodded again. Her reserve wasn't exactly cold, but Annie sensed she was someone who kept her distance from strangers. Annie wondered if she should just move on and stop bothering the woman, when Ms. Booth said, "You're Judy Holden's daughter?"

Annie smiled in surprise. "Now, that's a first. People usually ask if I'm Betsy Holden's granddaughter. I guess there aren't as many people in Stony Point who remember my mom. Did you know her?"

"A bit," the older woman said hesitantly. "I went to school with Judy a long time ago. She was actually a grade below mine. Didn't I hear she married a missionary?"

"Yes, she married George Spencer soon after he visited the church here," Annie said. She looked at the quiet woman closely, wondering if Josephine Booth could possibly be the Jo from her mother's journal. She was the first person Annie had met in Stony Point who remembered her mother, and her name just happened to be Josephine? Surely, it wasn't a coincidence.

"That's nice," Ms. Booth said vaguely, pulling Annie back to the conversation. "I hope they're both well."

"They died," Annie said softly. "Quite a few years ago."

"Oh, I'm sorry," the older woman said, and Annie was alarmed to see her face grow pale. She put a trembling hand to her cheek. "I'm afraid I didn't keep up. I always pictured Judy off in some wild place, teaching and having her adventures."

"That's all right," Annie said gently. "Mom was doing what she loved most in the world. She caught tuberculosis in Africa, and she insisted on staying there and continuing the work. She couldn't leave behind the people she'd come to love. My dad passed soon after Mom. He had a stroke, but I think he also had a broken heart. They were very close." She looked closely at the tall woman who still seemed shaken. "Are you feeling all right?"

"I'll be fine. I am a bit hypoglycemic, and I need to stop and have a snack soon," Ms. Booth said, forcing a tight smile. "It was nice meeting you and hearing about your mother. As I said, I only knew her slightly." The older woman turned her eyes back to the pile of books, effectively shutting Annie out.

"Right, of course," Annie answered, taking a step back from the counter. She felt a small flutter of disappointment. This stiff woman couldn't possibly be the wild, passionate Jo from her mother's journal. Annie murmured something vaguely polite and backed away from the desk to head for the Reference Room.

She slipped through the archway and into the Reference Room. The reference books stood in neat rows on the shelves that lined one wall. The other wall was lined with computer stations. Since it was still early, the normally busy computers were mostly empty.

As Annie walked by one woman staring intently at a screen, she peeked over her shoulder. The woman was looking intently at something called Facebook. During one of LeeAnn's pitches about the value of joining the information age, Annie was certain Facebook had come up at some point.

To Annie's surprise, she recognized the only other computer user. It was Mackenzie slouching in the computer chair with a frown on her face.

"Good morning, Mackenzie," Annie said.

The teenager sat up sharply. "Good morning, Mrs. Dawson."

"I'm surprised you didn't sleep in this morning after so much excitement last night."

Mackenzie sighed. "I'm making a list of the possible things Vanessa and I could volunteer for. I couldn't use my laptop because Mom took it. She caught me last night, and now I'm grounded except for school and the library, *and* I still have to do the mayor's service work."

Annie winced. "You might have fun working with Vanessa."

"If I do," Mackenzie said glumly, "it'll be the only fun I have for a long time."

Annie patted the girl on the shoulder as she turned back to her screen. She felt bad for Mackenzie, but when Annie thought back to her own teen escapades with Alice, she didn't get away with much either. Sometimes Annie suspected Gram had some kind of magical power. It wasn't until LeeAnn hit her teens that Annie realized she probably hadn't been as sneaky as she thought she was. Usually Annie took one look at LeeAnn's face and knew when her daughter was up to something.

She headed for the bulky microfiche reader that sat close to the main stacks of the reference section. It looked ancient and hulking next to the streamlined computers, and Annie patted it gently. *We old dinosaurs have to stick together*, she thought fondly. Then she glanced down the stacks. Maybe she'd take just one more minute.

She walked down the row of books to the back wall, and then slipped along the wall where a familiar piece of framed art called to her. It was one of Gram's Betsy Original cross-stitch landscapes. This one featured Butler's Lighthouse, but not as the scary source of ghost legends. In Gram's cross-stitch seascape, the lighthouse stood soldier straight at the end of the point, its light bathing the picture in gold. The lighthouse looked like a guardian and protector, guiding ships to safety. Annie took a moment to absorb her grandmother's bright optimism. All of the Betsy Originals that Annie had seen conveyed that same quality of hope and warmth.

Annie knew that the edifice that inspired the cross-stitch scene had taken the life of a sailor aboard a fishing boat in a storm. Gram hadn't focused on the loss, but on those saved. The lighthouse wasn't a reminder of a killing storm, but a guardian that brought men safely home.

"We have to stop meeting like this," a cheery voice said behind Annie. She turned to face Grace's sweet smile.

"I just needed a reminder of Gram's vision," Annie said. "Sometimes it's too easy to focus on the negative things in life and the unanswered questions. Gram always seemed to look for the light."

Grace nodded, her own face solemn for a moment, and Annie wondered if she had accidentally reminded the librarian of her grief over her deceased husband. But Grace turned to her with a smile, "Do you need any help today?"

"No, I'm going through the newspaper microfiche again."

"Well, you're certainly a pro at that. I should have you give lessons. Some of our patrons act like the old microfiche viewer might explode if they get too close," Grace said. "Well, if you're all set, I'm going to lend a hand in creating the toy display."

"Oh, really? I've been looking forward to seeing that."

"You'll have to take a peek before you leave," Grace said. "I'm going to get Josephine to help me as soon as Valerie gets back from her break. Josephine has a wonderful eye for composition. We get her to do all the displays."

"I'm looking forward to it," Annie said. She took one last look at Gram's beautiful cross-stitch, and then headed back to the microfiche reader. It was time to poke into the past again.

She retrieved the newspaper microfiche for the oldest year her mom could possibly have entertained thoughts of a cute boy and threaded it into the reader. She learned a tourist swore he'd seen a mermaid sunning herself on a rock in the harbor. This report was followed by a flurry of letters to the editor from fishermen talking about the mermaids they'd caught or nearly caught.

She saw the high school had an unusually good year in sports. She learned that Town Hall got a new paint job. But she found nothing about an accident on the lighthouse road so she swapped the microfiche for the next one and then the next one.

As always, dipping into the day-to-day history of Stony Point fascinated her, but this time she paused frequently to picture her mom as a young girl attending each community event. She knew her mother loved the beach from the words she'd read in her journal, but each page of *The Point* brought up a new question. Did her mother love parades? Did she find the loud boom of the fireworks a little unnerving, as Annie sometimes did? Did the National Anthem make her cry?

Annie felt like she'd gotten the barest glimpse into her mother through the journal, and now she wanted to know so much more. She had questions on top of questions and no one to ask. She blinked back tears as she slipped another sheet of microfiche into the viewer. Then she froze, staring at the screen. She'd found it.

*A Stony Point girl has died from a fall from the cliffs bordering the access road to Butler's Lighthouse.*

*Chief Carson Edwards of the Stony Point police department reports that 11-year-old Jenny Matthews died of injuries sustained in the fall. Edwards says the child was walking on the road with two companions in the storm at about 8:30 p.m. He also reports the accident ties into the lighthouse legend that has caused that strip of road to be a popular spot among Stony Point teens.*

*According to a Stony Point resident, who preferred not to be named, "The Butler's Lighthouse legend states that a previous lighthouse keeper placed a curse on the children of Stony Point. Anyone who touches the lighthouse in a storm will be visited by ghosts." For generations, this promise of ghosts has brought young people up the narrow road to prove their courage, to respond to a dare, or simply for a chance to see ghosts.*

*"The legend is just foolishness. That road is slick as glass in the rain," Chief Edwards says. "I hope we can learn from this horrible tragedy so we don't lose any more of Stony Point's children. Nobody belongs out there in that kind of weather."*

*The police department refused to release the names of Jenny Matthew's two companions. Her parents refused to comment. A friend of the family told this reporter that Jenny will be buried in a private ceremony—no obituary will be published. The family asks that donations to charity be made in lieu of flowers.*

With a shaking hand, Annie pressed the button to print out a copy of the story on the screen. She now knew what happened to little Jenny. She'd panicked in the dark storm and died. Annie couldn't imagine what that must have done to the child's parents and to her sister.

She folded the sheet of paper carefully and slipped it into her crocheted bag. Then she rolled the microfiche out of the machine and returned it carefully to its small box. In her heart, Annie had known the girls' adventure had ended tragically, but seeing the story in stark words on the screen had made everything seem so much more real.

As she slipped the handful of microfiche rolls back into the storage cabinet, she was startled by a shout from the front of the library. She rushed through the stacks to find Valerie Duffy pounding the buttons on a phone behind the circulation desk. She looked up at Annie, her eyes panicky. "Do you have a cell phone? Our phones are still out from the storm last night."

Annie nodded and fished the phone out of her bag. "Call 911!" Valerie urgently cried. "Josephine has collapsed in the children's room!"

# ~18~

nnie punched the numbers and handed the phone to Valerie so she could talk the operator through the particulars. Then she followed Valerie back to the children's area.

Ms. Booth lay on the floor beside the big freestanding glass case. Two cardboard boxes of toys sat near her, and Grace knelt at her side. She looked up and said, "Annie, could you bring me a couple of the cushions from the children's area?"

Annie hurried over and grabbed two of the bright round cushions the small children sat on during story time. When she hurried back, Grace crammed the cushions under Josephine's legs to elevate them, and then she turned to Valerie who still held Annie's cell phone to her ear. "Tell them her pulse is steady at eighty," Grace said.

Valerie nodded and repeated the information. Then Grace turned back to Annie. "I think someone left a small afghan back in the workroom." She gestured toward the door behind the librarian's desk. "Could you get it, please?"

Annie nodded, glad to have something to do. Behind her she could hear Grace's capable tone as she passed along information about Josephine's respiration. Annie's eyes scanned the floor as she walked. A teddy bear lay sprawled with its rump in the air near the base of the glass display.

The room behind the librarian's desk was small, but it held several worn padded chairs and a coffeepot on the corner of a metal desk. Piles of books were tucked in each corner. Annie spotted a soft blue afghan draped over a chair and carried it back to spread over the unconscious woman.

Grace shifted position to make room, and Annie saw that a toy had been hidden behind Grace's bent figure. The rag doll from Grey Gables lay near Josephine Booth's shoulder. Could the doll be related to the older woman's collapse, or was Annie's imagination running away with her again?

Annie concentrated on staying out of the way as Grace took charge of the situation. She sent Valerie back out to man the front desk and watch for the ambulance. Then she asked Annie if she could gather up any scattered toys and put them back into the cardboard boxes.

"We don't want anyone to trip over them," Grace said, her eyes never leaving Josephine's still face. "And since the toys are on loan, I don't want any of the children playing with them later today during story time."

Annie picked up the teddy bear and the battered rag doll and slipped them into the box. Then she carried the boxes over to tuck them behind the children's librarian's desk.

"Has Ms. Booth been sick?" she asked quietly.

"I don't think so," Grace said. "She's a bit hypoglycemic, but that's the only thing she's ever mentioned. Normally she's very careful not to get too shaky, though I tend to nag her about snacks just to be sure." Grace smiled slightly, but it slipped away quickly as she looked worriedly at Josephine's still face. "I had carried the first box of toys in so she could get started with the display. Usually it's better if Valerie and

I just hand her things and let her work her magic over these displays. She really has the eye of an artist." Grace seemed to realize she was rambling. She adjusted the edge of the afghan over Ms. Booth's arm. "I was just getting the second box when I heard the crash. I found her on the floor. I suspect she fainted, but it looks like she may have struck her head as she fell. It's a bit worrying, though her pupils look fine." Grace gently lifted the unconscious woman's hair away from her face, and Annie could see the purplish swelling on the woman's forehead.

"You're certainly handling this well," Annie said. "I think I would have panicked."

"Don and I were both EMTs with the volunteer fire department here for years. He loved helping people," she said, her voice slightly rough. "I quit when he died, but I suppose it's not something you forget."

Their conversation was cut off by the arrival of the ambulance crew. Two men brought in a stretcher piled with equipment. They shooed Grace and Annie both away and bent over the unconscious woman. Shortly after they began their examination, the older woman's eyes fluttered and opened.

"Ms. Booth?" the technician said loudly. "Can you hear me?"

"Yes, I'm not deaf," Josephine said as she struggled to sit up. "What happened?"

"Please, just lie back," the EMT said, pushing against her shoulders gently. "You fell and hit your head. Do you remember that?"

The older woman reached a trembling hand up to touch

her forehead, but the technician pushed it away. "We're going to take you to the hospital to get you checked out," he said.

"Oh, don't be silly," Ms. Booth said, her voice slightly stronger. "I don't need to go to the hospital. I just got a little dizzy. I'm hypoglycemic."

"We insist," the EMT said. "You could have a concussion. And we really need to be certain your dizzy spell wasn't caused by something more serious."

She voiced a few more objections in her high thin voice, but the young men loaded her efficiently onto the stretcher and wheeled her out of the library. Grace caught them just at the arch that marked the entrance to the children's section and lay a gentle hand on the library volunteer's shoulder. "I'll come by and see you soon."

"Good," the woman answered, showing more spirit than Annie would have guessed from their earlier conversation. "You can drive me home."

Then, just before they wheeled her beyond hearing, Annie was sure she heard Ms. Booth say something about a doll. Annie hurried after the technicians, but they quickly stowed the stretcher onto the ambulance and practically slammed the doors in Annie's face.

Annie walked back into the library and crossed the main room to the children's room. Slipping behind the librarian's desk, she grabbed the rag doll from the box. She smoothed the faded dress and imagined little Jenny clinging to her doll in the storm. Then she carried it to the front desk where Valerie stood beside Grace.

"I'm going to take this doll with me if you don't mind," Annie said. "I found a reference to it in a journal of my mother's. I think I need to find out some more about it."

"No problem," Grace answered. "We have two boxes of stuff. I have no idea how we're going to fit everything in. Especially without Josephine's help."

"Maybe we could just wait until Josephine comes back?" Valerie said tentatively, her voice anxious. "You don't think she's going to be out long, do you?"

"I'm sure she'll be fine," Grace said, patting the other woman on the arm. "But you have to be careful with head injuries. It's a good sign that she regained consciousness before they took her to the hospital. The longer you're out, the worse the injury is most of the time."

"Do you think they'll keep her overnight?" Annie asked.

"At her age, I'm sure of it," Grace said. "It's just safer. Why?"

"I thought I might go by and visit later. Josephine knew my mother. I think it's something my mom would have done."

Grace smiled at Annie warmly. "That's a terrific idea. I'm sure Josephine would love it. She doesn't have any family around here anymore. I'll be popping by this evening too."

Annie carried the rag doll out into the sunshine. Something inside her was certain that Josephine Booth was Jo Matthews, her mother's best friend and Jenny's sister. If that was true, Annie wasn't sure how much the older woman would appreciate her digging up the past.

Still feeling a bit shaky, Annie decided she needed to sit down and sort out her feelings before she tried driving home. She thought about putting the doll in her car before heading to the diner, but somehow she didn't really want to be parted from it. Though it was Jenny's doll, her mother had rescued it, and now Annie felt that connection to her mother when she looked at it.

As she pushed open the door to The Cup & Saucer, the cowbell over the door clanged a welcome. The smell of coffee and bacon wrapped around her like a memory of home, and Annie instantly felt her spirits lift a little. She looked over the crowded room but didn't spot anyone she knew well, which was fine. She needed a minute to herself after the library emergency.

She caught sight of Peggy gesturing toward an empty table near the front windows. Annie nodded and headed that way. As Annie slipped into the padded booth seat, Peggy flipped over the coffee mug, but Annie held up her hand.

"I don't think I want coffee this time," Annie said. "I need something calming."

Peggy's brown eyes opened wide, curiosity crackling. "How about some herbal tea? Chamomile is supposed to be calming." She leaned forward and added in a whisper, "It always tastes like medicine to me, but some people really like it."

Her friend's bluntness coaxed a smile from Annie. "Since you make it sound so good, I'd like a cup, please."

"Coming right up." Peggy bent closer to the table for a moment. "I saw the ambulance go by and stop at the library. Do you know what happened?"

"One of the volunteers is hypoglycemic," Annie said. She knew there was no way to head off the town's gossip train for the sake of Josephine's privacy, but perhaps she could blunt it a bit. "She fainted."

"Oh, I hope she'll be all right," Peggy said, concern clear on her face.

"I think she's going to be fine. She was conscious when they took her to the hospital," Annie said. "I got the feeling it was more of a precaution."

Peggy's eyes wandered toward the kitchen where her boss was looking pointedly at them. "OK, tea's coming up!" she sang out before hurrying away.

Annie folded her hands on the table and stared out the large window. She saw two young women in the bright colors that seemed to be part of the uniform of Stony Point tourists. The women stood in front of Dress to Impress, gesturing toward the display. Annie knew the dress shop was featuring sundresses to welcome in the warmer weather. She'd spent some time gazing at them herself, trying to decide if she needed one more dress in her closet, considering she spent more time digging around in the attic, gardening, or even slopping through mud than she spent at fancy events.

Had she really left behind the days of fussing over just the right look, or had she merely traded it in for butting into other people's lives? Sometimes she felt that her little mysteries were nothing more than that—forcing herself on people who wanted the past to stay silent and buried. Would Josephine Booth feel that way? Annie wondered if her time in Stony Point was accomplishing anything positive.

Annie's hand strayed over to fuss with the hem of the doll's dress. This mystery had given her a glimpse of her mother, and for that she was grateful. For the first time, she really felt she had some things in common with her mother. The journal had changed Annie's perception of her mother from being a near stranger that Annie held in awe, to a girl with a long, blond ponytail and a deep love for her friends.

How could she regret learning that?

She barely glanced up as Peggy filled her mug with hot water and laid the tea bag beside it. "Are you all right, Annie?" Peggy asked, and this time Annie heard only concern instead of curiosity in the young woman's voice.

"I'll be fine," Annie said, smiling. "I think I might like some buttered toast to go with this tea."

"Coming right up," Peggy sang out as she turned to head back to the kitchen.

Annie held the tea up and sniffed the mildly grassy scent. Her eyes turned to the window again as she sipped, deep in thought again. Her mind drifted back to the cool reception she'd gotten when she first came back to Stony Point. She knew Stella Brickson, especially, was certain Annie had come to meddle and pry. Maybe Stella was more right than she knew. Maybe all Annie did was meddle.

She looked up as Peggy laid the toast on the table in front of her. "I just wanted to say that Wally has been glowing ever since we dropped off the boat. I don't know that I've ever seen him so proud. He likes doing all the handyman projects, but making something like that—something that came out of his head and his hands—I think that's the happiest I've seen him outside of fishing. Thank you, Annie." She patted Annie's arm, and then hurried over to the next table where a man in a flannel shirt was waving his bill at her.

Annie smiled after her. *Is that some kind of sign?* she asked God in her head. She turned to look toward the door as the cowbell drew her attention. Alice and Jim stood just inside the door, scanning the crowd. Annie waved at them, and they headed for her table. The bounce in Alice's step made her almost seem to be levitating.

"Wasn't last night amazing?" Alice asked as she slipped into the booth across from Annie.

"It was terrifying and wet," Annie said, agreeably. "The rental car people are going to love you for turning the car into a wading pool, Jim."

"The rental car people often have complaints about the state of the cars I use. I'm used to it. I figure if it's still driv-able when I'm done with it, they've come out ahead." Jim levered himself down onto the seat beside Alice, using his cane for the awkward maneuver. Then he turned his rak-ish grin on Annie. "So, is the mayor still furious with me? I thought he might knock my head off last night."

"Poor Jim," Alice said, giving his bicep a squeeze. "I tried to tell Ian it was all my idea, but I guess it wouldn't feel the same to loom over me muttering threats."

Annie's eyes grew wide. "Ian threatened you?"

Jim shook his head. "Alice is being dramatic. No threats." Then he added with a chuckle. "Plenty of looming though. He was just being protective of his lady. I can respect that."

"Ian and I are only friends," Annie said firmly.

"Right," Alice said agreeably, looking out the window to hide the smile tugging at the corners of her mouth.

"Just like Alice and I," Jim added.

"Really?" Alice said, turning to slip an arm through his and lean into him. "Would you beat someone up over me? Huh? Huh?"

"You know it, Gorgeous," Jim answered, putting on his best Chicago gangster accent.

"Really, you two," Annie said. "Ian and I *are* just friends."

"Someone should tell Ian that," Jim said agreeably. "Before he rides his white horse all over someone for your sake."

Annie tried again to insist that Ian did not have romantic feelings for her, but the discussion was interrupted by another visit from Peggy to take the newcomers' orders. Annie definitely didn't want to talk about the mayor in front of Peggy. She'd never squelch the rumors that would spring up.

Alice and Jim had clearly come in hungry as they both ordered big breakfasts with pancakes, eggs, and sausage.

"Sleuthing makes me hungry," Alice said when she caught Annie's look.

"Have you been sleuthing this morning?" Annie asked.

Alice shook her head. "It's left over from last night. Delayed sleuthing starvation. It's a clinical disorder. I saw it on television."

Annie laughed at Alice's cheerful silliness. Clearly Jim Parker made her happy. Alice had always been ready for a good adventure, but Annie had sensed sadness in her as well. She knew Alice's divorce had left scars. Sometimes Alice's smiles held a melancholy edge, but not today. Today her friend glowed, and from the warm looks Jim turned her way regularly, Annie suspected Alice might have said yes to his invitation to follow him out West.

She felt a pang at that thought. She wasn't ready to lose her best friend after just barely reconnecting again. She pushed that idea down as selfish and forced a smile. "So, what are you two planning for today?"

"Well, I have all the photos I need for this lighthouse," Jim said. "So basically my job here is done as soon as I track down the information about the little girl who died on the cliffs. I haven't given up on that."

"Oh," Annie said softly. "I have that information." She shifted the doll from the top of her purse and rifled through until she found the folded copier paper. She handed it to Jim.

Jim and Alice read it together, heads nearly touching. "Wow, so the little girl in your mother's journal was the little girl who died," Alice said. "Jenny, right?"

Annie nodded. "And I think I know who Jo is."

Alice's eyebrows climbed in interest.

"I met Josephine Booth this morning at the library, and she said she'd gone to school with my mother. Obviously, Jo is a shortened form of Josephine, though it doesn't sound like she goes by it anymore. The women at the library definitely call her Josephine."

"Well, I'd certainly say that seems like a strong possibility," Jim said. "But it could just be a coincidence. Sometimes a given name can be very popular in a specific geographic region. You wouldn't believe how many guys named Jim I went to school with."

"That's not my only clue," Annie said. She picked up the doll and held it as she spoke. "As I was finishing up in the Reference Room, I heard someone call out from the front desk. Josephine had collapsed in the children's room while she was setting up the old toys display. This doll—Jenny's doll—lay beside her on the floor."

"Is she going to be OK?" Alice asked.

"Grace seemed to think so," Annie said. "Apparently

Josephine is hypoglycemic. She mentioned it when I was talking to her, and she seemed a little shaky. So it might have been another coincidence that she happened to be holding this doll when she collapsed, but it also might be the doll that brought it on."

"Sounds like you're not quite done with the mysteries," Alice said.

Annie sighed. "Maybe I should be. If Josephine is Jo, then maybe she doesn't want to have her little sister's death dug up and put in a book. If the past is too painful, doesn't she have a right to keep her own secrets?"

Alice shrugged. "I don't know. Do you think you can just walk away and not know?"

"Look," Jim said, "I think we need to ask the woman. I don't want to include anything in the book that's going to hurt someone. I can leave Jenny out entirely or put a vague reference that doesn't reveal anything. I want to make the best book possible, but not at the expense of real people. That's not how I work."

Annie reached over and rested her hand briefly on Jim's. "I'm glad to hear that."

"So it sounds like we need to make a trip to the hospital," Alice said. "Then we'll just leave it up to Josephine."

Annie nodded as Peggy showed up with loaded plates. As Peggy set the plates in front of Jim and Alice, Annie's eyes turned back to the window. A cloud passed in front of the sun just as she looked out, throwing the street in a brief shadow. Annie shivered, hoping that wasn't a premonition of the confrontation that lay in front of her.

# ~19~

After the food arrived, discussion turned to more pleasant subjects, or at least different ones. Jim launched into stories about some of the Northwest lighthouses.

"Off the coast of Oregon," Jim said, "there is a lighthouse that sits on a hunk of basalt rock right out in the water. The coastline gets so foggy, they decided that putting a lighthouse out in the water was the best idea. Unfortunately, that hunk of rock was cursed."

"Oh," Alice said, as she nibbled her bacon. "A curse?"

"The native people of the area said evil spirits lived on the rock. And apparently just building the thing helped stock it with ghosts. The surveyor for the site drowned. It wasn't exactly an auspicious beginning. Apparently more workmen died during construction."

"So those would all be pre-lighthouse ghosts," Alice said.

"But still fierce ones," Jim said. "Anyway, they had to send lighthouse keepers out there for only a few months at a time. One guy who stayed a little too long went crazy from the loneliness ... or maybe from something else."

"Sounds like a fun place for a vacation," Alice said.

"If you come with me," Jim said, "I'll show you all the best spots."

Alice laughed at that, and Annie felt a small gush of relief followed by guilt. Apparently Alice hadn't made up her mind yet, and even though Annie wanted her friend to be happy, it was hard not to hope her final answer would be no.

Jim was an excellent storyteller, but Annie still found her mind wandering more and more as he talked. She knew she needed to give Josephine Booth time to settle in at the hospital, but she was eager to get the meeting with the woman over with, before her nerves grew any worse.

Alice laid her fork down on her empty plate with the small ringing sound of metal on china. "I think we lost Annie."

Annie looked up sharply at the sound of her name. "I'm sorry. I guess I'm just worried about Ms. Booth."

"Why don't you ladies head on over and see if you can visit with her," Jim said. "I suspect she'll be more open to a visit from two lovely ladies than from a ruffian like me. Let me know what she wants to do about Jenny, if indeed she was her sister."

"We will," Alice said.

Jim stood to let Alice out of the booth, and Annie stood up, reaching into her purse for money to pay her check. "Don't bother with that," Jim said. "I'll take care of the check after I have a slice of pie."

"Pie for breakfast?" Annie said.

Jim shrugged. "It's fruit. Fruit makes a healthy breakfast food."

"Don't get him started," Alice said, "or he'll tell you why chocolate cake makes a great lunch."

"I don't remember you arguing too hard about that one yesterday at lunch," Jim reminded her.

Alice laughed and shook her head. She gave Jim a quick peck on the cheek and whispered something in his ear before leading the way out of the diner. Annie caught sight of Peggy grinning from ear to ear and knew the curious waitress had caught that little public display of affection.

"Shall we take my car or yours?" Alice asked.

"Let's take yours," Annie said. "I'm a little too distracted to drive. And I'm getting used to the feeling of wind in my hair."

"We'll make an adventurer out of you yet, Annie Dawson," Alice said, giving her friend a quick hug.

The drive to the hospital was smooth; tourist traffic hadn't yet begun to clog up the roads with people unsure of the area. Annie enjoyed looking at the houses they passed with their tidy yards and bright spring flowers. After a few minutes, she turned to Alice. "Have you decided if you're going with Jim?"

"Are we talking about the high school version of 'going with?'" Alice asked innocently.

"Actually, I'm talking about whether you're leaving with him for the West Coast."

Alice flashed her a wicked grin. "Have *you* decided if you're going to stay in Texas when you go back for the birthday party?"

Annie groaned. "Not completely. One minute I'm sure I belong here. Then something happens, and I wonder … "

"Wonder what?" Alice asked when Annie let the sentence drop.

"Wonder if I've made more trouble than I'm worth since I got here," Annie said. "All I seem to do is poke into hornets' nests. Stella was ready to have me flogged for asking questions the first week I got here, if she could have found someone still handing out public floggings. Harry Stevens practically dropped a boulder on my head to keep me out of his family's business. And now I may have put poor Josephine Booth in the hospital."

"First of all, Stella is now delighted that you brought her past out in the open so she could heal," Alice said. "And with Ian's help, you brought honor back to Harry's family. And *finally*, you don't even know for sure that Ms. Booth's collapse had anything to do with you. The poor woman might have just needed a sandwich."

Annie blinked back tears and looked rigidly at the road ahead. "We don't know that I didn't cause her collapse either."

"Annie," Alice said gently, "sometimes you have to clean out a wound to get it to heal, and while that's never pleasant, you've helped put a lot of people on the road to healing since you got here. You have nothing to feel guilty about."

*Except maybe Josephine Booth*, Annie thought, but she didn't say anything.

Alice pulled into the parking lot of the small brick hospital and quickly found a parking space in the visitor's lot. Annie tucked the rag doll into her purse and followed Alice's focused stride across the smooth asphalt and through the huge sliding doors.

Two elderly ladies in pink sat behind the front information desk. The smaller of the two looked up at Annie and Alice with eager eyes. "May we help you?" she asked in a cheerful chirp.

"Yes," Alice said. "We're here to visit Josephine Booth. She came in this morning."

The woman smiled and turned to squint at the computer screen. She pecked at a few keys nervously, as if she was unsure of what the computer might do in response. Finally, she said, "Room 214. You'll find the elevator right down this hall and to the right."

"Thank you," Annie said as Alice began a quick walk to the elevator. She nearly had to trot to catch up. "Alice, when did this become a race?"

"I thought a brisk approach would keep you from thinking too much," Alice said. "How's it working?"

"Pretty well, assuming I don't collapse in a heap and end up in an adjoining room to Ms. Booth."

"Think of how much the two of you could talk then."

But Alice relented and slowed down to a more normal pace, giving Annie a chance to look around. She'd rarely been to the hospital here. The building was old, and the brick walls had the softened edges of many layers of paint. Right now everything was painted a cheerful pale blue. Along the wall, she saw framed photos of lobster boats bobbing next to weathered docks interspersed among lovely pieces of antique needlework, also framed.

The carpet was a lovely dark blue-green and looked new, but when they reached the elevator, Annie could see the building's age again in the ancient doors that opened with an ominous rumble. Once inside, they lurched up to the second floor and waited an unusually long time for the doors to finally heave open again. Annie decided she might use the stairs on the way out.

The door to Room 214 stood open. Annie peeked inside and saw the white-haired woman alone in the room, sitting upright in her hospital bed with the covers folded neatly down to her lap. She stared out the window near the bed and only turned to face them when Annie knocked.

"Yes?" the older woman said, looking at Annie and Alice curiously.

"Hi, I'm Annie Dawson. We met at the library this morning. I was still in the library when you had your accident, and I wanted to stop by and see if you needed anything." She took a hesitant step into the room. "This is my friend, Alice MacFarlane."

Alice nodded and mumbled something polite, clearly leaving the conversation to Annie.

"That's very kind of you both," Ms. Booth said politely. "Please come in. They've told me I have to stay here overnight for observation. That's so silly. I'm just fine."

"I'm glad to hear that," Annie said.

Annie walked across the room quickly, and the two women looked at one another awkwardly for a moment. "I have a question to ask you," Annie said.

Josephine folded her hands in her lap and nodded.

"Were you one of the Wild Jays?" Annie asked.

Josephine Booth winced, and then nodded her head with a small smile. "I haven't heard those words in many years."

"So you were?" Annie said. "You were my mother's best friend, Jo?"

Tears filled the old woman's eyes. "I don't know that your mother would have described me that way. I was very unkind to her once."

"She described you exactly that way," Annie said. "I've read her journal." Then she gently slipped the rag doll from her purse. "Is this what upset you at the library?"

Josephine Booth reached out a trembling hand to touch the hem of the doll's dress, then let her hand drop back into her lap. "Matilda. Where did you find her?"

"My mother put her in Gram's attic," Annie said. "In her journal, she said she was going to keep her for you, in case you ever decided you wanted her."

"That sounds like Judy," the old woman said. "She wouldn't believe there might be something a person just never gets over. She was always trying to make things better."

"I know about Jenny's accident," Alice whispered.

"It should never have happened," Josephine said. "I was the big sister. I was supposed to watch out for her." She turned away toward the window again as tears ran down her face. "I failed her."

"You weren't much more than a child yourself," Annie said, "and you were doing something teens have done for a long time. The mayor caught two girls up there just last night. You couldn't have known what would happen."

"I should have!" Josephine repeated stubbornly. "I should have kept her safe. I … I laughed at her for being afraid."

"I have a little sister," Alice said gently, stepping up beside Annie. "She always wanted to tag along with me, and I teased her terribly for being little and scared sometimes. That's what big sisters *do*. You couldn't have known how it would end. You didn't do anything we haven't all done— make a mistake."

"My mother never forgave me," Josephine said, "and she never got over it."

"That still doesn't make it your fault," Alice said.

"It wasn't Judy's fault either," Josephine whispered. "But I blamed her. I said horrible things to her. After that, I couldn't even think about her without reliving that night." She looked at Annie. "Does Judy's journal say if she ever forgave me?"

"She was never angry with you," Annie said. "She just hurt for you. She felt guilty and sad that she couldn't help."

Josephine nodded. "I think I might like to keep Jenny's doll."

Annie handed it to her, and the older woman straightened the doll's long thick hair gently. "Our Nona—our grandmother—made this for Jenny. Jenny was her favorite. She always said I was too noisy and too bold."

"My mother admired your boldness tremendously," Annie said. "You know, a horrible accident leaves everyone involved with pain, plagued by thoughts of what they should have done. She felt that way too. She felt like she'd failed you."

Josephine Booth nodded sadly with her eyes on the little doll. "Once this doll represented everything I thought I didn't have. I wasn't the favorite of my grandmother. Then, it was just a reminder of my loss. Now, I think I can see why Jenny loved this little doll so much. When she held it, it reminded Jenny that she was truly and deeply loved. Now it can remind me of how much I loved my little sister." Her voice grew ragged and she whispered, "And how much I miss her."

Annie squeezed the old woman's hand. "I'm so sorry."

Josephine nodded, her eyes still on the rag doll. She tugged at the apron, and then pointed at the ragged embroidery. "I did that." She looked up at Annie. "Your grandfather called Judy and me 'Wild Jays' because our names both started with J and because of the wild schemes we got into. Most of them were my ideas, but Judy could hold her own. We got into trouble together from the time we were little. Did your mother's journal say how we met?"

Annie shook her head.

"There was a new child at school. He was in my class, but I didn't pay him much attention. Some of the other boys were picking on him one day, knocking his books on the ground and pushing him. Judy marched right up to them—and she was just a first grader. She got in their faces and told them that being bullies shamed their mamas." Josephine smiled and shook her head. "A couple of the boys backed down. But the biggest one—he didn't like being scolded by a little girl. He gave her a push and yelled at her. So I knocked him down and made him eat dirt."

"Good for you," Alice said.

"I was tall for my age," Josephine said a bit sheepishly. "And you know what Judy did?"

Annie and Alice shook their heads.

"She told me that I shouldn't fight. Then she gave me the cupcake her mother had put in her lunch. We were best friends from that moment on." Josephine looked into Annie's eyes. "I loved your mother."

"And she loved you," Annie said.

The older woman blinked away tears and turned her eyes back to the doll. "Judy and I made Jenny an honorary

Wild Jay," Josephine said. "I embroidered that on the apron as proof."

"That probably made Jenny very happy."

The older woman nodded, and her tear-filled eyes dropped to the doll again. "But I think it also made her feel like she had to live up to us. Be just as brave. Be just as foolish. She fixated on the lighthouse because it seemed like the bravest thing anyone could do."

The room fell quiet as the older woman slipped away into her memories. Finally, Annie laid a gentle hand on her arm. "We should go and let you rest."

Josephine looked up, startled. She'd forgotten them. "Maybe we could talk again sometime. I would like to tell you more about your mother."

"I would like that too," Annie said. "I loved my mother dearly, but I feel like I'm only just beginning to meet her."

"You're very much like her, I think," Josephine said. "I'll tell you stories. But I am feeling a little tired now."

"Of course," Annie said, backing away from the bed.

"Ms. Booth?" Alice said tentatively.

"Please call me Jo," the older woman said.

"Thank you. Annie and I have a friend. He's doing a book about the lighthouse and about the stories surrounding it. He knows about Jenny, but he doesn't want to do anything that would hurt anyone. Would you think about whether he could mention Jenny in the book?"

Jo looked at Alice and then Annie solemnly. "Do you trust this friend?"

Alice nodded. "He's a good person."

"Perhaps I could chat with him," Jo said. "Maybe it's

been too long since Jenny's been remembered. If he could tell it the right way."

"He would like to come and talk to you about it."

Jo smiled, and Annie could see how tired the old woman looked. "Good. Not tonight, though. I think I've had enough excitement for one day."

"No, not tonight," Alice agreed. Then she patted the old woman's hand and added. "I'm glad to have met you. Good night."

## ~ 20 ~

*T*he next few days passed quietly for Annie. She still felt a bit raw, and even though her "mystery" was technically over, she didn't feel settled. So she stayed close to Grey Gables and busied herself with little things while she thought. A couple of times she thought about driving into town and having a talk with Ian about their friendship, but finally decided to simply let it go.

She transplanted her flats of pansies into the wooden planters, and their bright little flower faces were only the tiniest bit downcast from the wait. Then she planted moss roses between the rocks that edged one corner of the huge yard.

As she slipped the delicate plants between the rocks, she marveled at the contrast between appearance and reality. *Moss roses look so fragile*, Annie thought, *but they flourish in the harshest spots in the garden.*

She thought about the moss roses on Gram's tea set. As a girl, the delicate-looking tea set had been the most beautiful thing she'd ever seen. She'd loved them so much that she made Alice use a mismatched cup and saucer she'd found, since her wild friend could be careless sometimes. Had Annie been valuing the wrong thing then?

Once or twice she wondered if Jim was still in town, or if he'd left with Alice. *Surely she would stop and say goodbye*, she thought.

One afternoon, she spent the better part of an hour sitting on the wide front porch with Boots in her lap. She gazed out at Butler's Lighthouse and thought about three girls losing themselves in the dark. The tragedy of Jenny dying was the most horrible loss, but her mother had also lost her best friend. And she suspected Jo had lost the most of all. She'd lost herself.

"Hello, stranger!"

Annie turned her head sharply. Alice strode across the long yard from the far side where the carriage house nestled among the trees. She carried her needlework tote and a breadbasket wrapped in embroidered tea towels. Annie smiled at her friend. "I don't know that I'm the one who's kept busy lately," she said.

Alice held up a hand. "Guilty as charged. And that's why I'm here." She sat down in the wicker chair next to Annie. Then she looked over the arm. "Is this the chair Wally fixed? It's really comfortable."

"It might be my new favorite," Annie said, then she gestured to the sleeping cat in her lap. "Boots was sleeping in it when I walked out here so I took this one, but I guess a warm lap trumps a new chair cushion."

Alice set the basket on the wicker table between them where a pitcher of iced tea already set between two glasses. "Two glasses?" Alice asked.

"I'm optimistic," Annie said. Then she laughed and confessed. "Actually, yesterday I only brought one and a bug flew into it. So I brought a backup today."

"*Ewww!*" Alice said, peering at the glasses. "Any bugs?"

"I don't think so."

Alice poured herself a glass of tea and offered Annie a muffin. "I finally made the blueberry-and-almond muffins I promised. They have a touch of lemon so they should be nice with the tea."

Annie took a bite of the warm muffin and savored the blend of favors. Alice was a wonder at baking. "So you're visiting and baking. How are you finding the time?"

"Jim finished the work he needed to do here and left for the West Coast," Alice said. Annie looked at her wide-eyed, but Alice kept talking before her friend could launch into a barrage of questions. "He talked to Ms. Booth, and she decided he could include Jenny's story as a kind of warning for young people about how dangerous legends can be—even without ghostly intervention. She even let him take a picture of Jenny's doll laying on a rock. The photo came out fantastic, sort of chilling and sad and ominous all at the same time. Maybe Ian should make that photo into posters for the high school. It might cut down on teens tromping up that road in a storm."

"Would it have kept you off the road?"

Alice thought about it for a moment, and then she shook her head. "No. I thought I was invincible."

"The teenage delusion," Annie agreed, leaning back.

"Jo asked me to tell you she's back at the library, and she'd love to get together to talk about your mom, whenever you want."

"I'd like that," Annie said.

"And speaking of the library," Alice held up the nee-dlework bag, "I've been spending so much time with Jim, I have barely even started on the little embroidered shoes.

I planned the design, but I was hoping you'd help me stitch it."

"I'm not anywhere near as good as you at embroidery," Annie protested.

"But you know all the stitches," Alice said. "I've seen you use them on some of the baby blankets you've crocheted. The embroidery you did on Joanna's sweater was lovely."

"Great big embroidery with yarn or silk ribbon," Annie said, "not itty-bitty embroidery with thread."

"It's the same technique," Alice insisted, "and I promised to bring the shoes to Mary Beth this afternoon. I'm sunk without you. *Please*." Alice stretched the word out until she sounded exactly like she did when they were kids, trying to talk Annie into some wild plan or other.

"I'll be glad to help," Annie said, "but let's take them inside. I don't want to chase bits of thread in the breeze."

Annie set Boots down on the porch, eliciting a disgruntled meow from the ball of gray fluff. Then they gathered their things and headed into the house with Boots stalking indignantly behind them.

They settled comfortably on the living room sofa, and Annie turned her attention to the tiny shoe. Alice was right. She'd done all of the basic embroidery stitches before in yarn when she'd embellished afghans and baby blankets, and in silk ribbon on Joanna's birthday sweater. Working with thread was just a bit more fidgety.

"You just have flowers and grasses on yours," Alice said. "I put the robin from the book on the tongue of this shoe. I was finishing up on the little guy this morning. That's when I realized I was never going to get these done in time." She held up her tiny shoe where a satin-stitch robin peered at them curiously.

"He looks just like I always imagined the robin in *The Secret Garden* would look," Annie said. "Like he's about to ask a question."

"Thanks," Alice said. "That's what I was going for. The robin was my favorite part of that book."

The two women worked quietly for a while until Annie felt more confident with her stitching. "So, Jim's gone, and you're still here," she said.

Alice looked up. "You're surprised?"

"A little," Annie admitted. "You two looked pretty cozy together."

"Jim is a fantastic guy, and it was really nice to be with someone who wasn't like ... " her voice trailed off as she bent her head over her stitching.

"Like John MacFarlane," Annie said carefully. She knew Alice's ex was still a touchy subject for her friend.

"Like him," Alice agreed. "But I'm really content here in Stony Point. I love my home. I enjoy my work, and I'm proud of the business I've built up. I have fantastic friends who are really more like family than my real family." She smiled warmly at Annie. "This is my home. As much as I enjoyed Jim's company and admire who he is, I'm not ready to give up *me* in order to chase after someone else's dreams. I liked having a man in my life, but I don't want to give up my life for a man. You know what I mean?"

Annie nodded. "I think so."

There was a long pause, and then Alice grinned at her. "But I have to tell you," she said, "if Jim were still in town, the library doll would just have to wear plain white shoes."

Annie laughed. "I'm glad to hear you still have your priorities in order."

"You know it," Alice said. Then she ducked her head back to her embroidery and asked, "Do you?"

"What do you mean?"

"Do you have *your* priorities in order?" Alice asked. "It's just that the twins' birthday party is awfully close. Do you know what you're going to do about Stony Point?"

Annie nodded. "I think so. I'm still getting my head around it, but I think so."

"You'll let me know when you get it settled?" Alice asked. "You know losing my best guy and my best friend in the same month would be tough on an old gal like me."

"Old?" Annie laughed at that. "Of all the many adjectives anyone would pick to describe Alice MacFarlane, old is not one of them." Then Annie added, "I'll let you know my decision soon. I have one more thing I have to check into."

Just then Boots' quizzical face appeared, peeking over the edge of the sofa. A furry paw darted out and snagged a skein of green floss before the cat took off. "Boots," Annie scolded, "we need that."

A minor chase around the living room followed that soon reduced both women to tears of laughter before Boots dropped the embroidery floss and raced out of the room in the direction of the kitchen. As they settled back down to finish the shoes, conversation stayed light and easy between them.

Finally, Annie finished the last stitch and carefully tied

off the thread on the inside of the shoe. "Done!"

"Great." Alice glanced at her watch. "And within the deadline. I'll just run these into Mary Beth's shop."

"I'd like to go with you," Annie said. "I think our mystery and this embroidery have inspired me. I have just enough time before I leave for Texas to make Joanna a rag doll to go with her birthday sweater. I've already finished a doll-sized sweater, but I'll need to pick up a skein of thick yarn for the hair and the fabric for the doll."

"That's a great idea."

"I also need to stop by Mr. Proctor's office," Annie said as she gathered her purse and slipped on some flats.

"The lawyer?"

Annie nodded. "I have some questions to ask him about an idea I'm considering. I've just been so caught up in the mystery; but I think Jenny's mystery might have helped me to solve another one."

"Oh?"

"The mystery of what I want."

## — 21 —

Though the beautifully decorated ranch house had large rooms, it seemed almost tiny when packed with ten rambunctious six-year-olds and assorted parents. Most of the adults clumped together in groups of two or three, and sipped lemonade from tall, narrow glasses while keeping sharp eyes on the children.

A little girl wearing a rose-color sweater over her blue sundress trotted across the large family room. Her silky blonde hair was pulled up into two pigtails that bounced as she walked. She reached the loveseat at the corner of the room and held up her new rag doll, her sparkling green eyes worried. "Could you tie Betsy's hair ribbon back, Gramma? My bows aren't as pretty as yours."

"I think you tie great bows," Annie said as she slipped the rose-color ribbon back through a hank of the doll's creamy yellow yarn hair. "Look how nice your sneakers look."

Joanna leaned close and whispered, "Mama tied them."

"You know, sweetie," Annie said as she looked at the little girl's pink face, "you don't have to wear that sweater now. It's a little hot for it."

Joanna looked horrified at the suggestion that she take off her new sweater. "It makes me and Betsy match!" Then she gave her grandmother a delicate kiss on the cheek, followed by one from Betsy, and marched back to where the girl half of the birthday party was gathered. The girls were having pretend tea with the moss-rose tea set Annie had given Joanna as a gift from her Great-Great-Grandma Betsy. So far, the tea set was holding up very well.

Annie suspected that the gift of the tea set had inspired the rag doll's name. Annie thought of how happy it would make Gram to see her doll-loving great-great-granddaughter sitting down to the tea party. "I guess it skips a few generations sometimes, Gram," Annie whispered as she watched Joanna set the doll carefully on a small chair and offer her a sip from the delicate-looking teacup.

"Mrs. Dawson, could you tell me where you got that darling boat?"

Annie turned to face a young woman with a round cheerful face and a stylish blue dress. "A friend in Stony Point made if for me," Annie said.

"Do you think your friend would take orders?" the woman asked. "My Andre said he wanted one for his birthday. It's at the end of summer. Do you think I could get one?"

"I wouldn't be surprised," Annie said. "It's all handmade though, so it's quite pricey."

The young woman waved that away. "Quality is worth the price. Does the artist have a website?"

Annie laughed aloud. "No, I don't think he even has a computer, but I'm not sure. If you'll write down your name and number, I'll give you a call when I get back to Stony Point and give you all the information about the boat."

"That would be wonderful," the woman gushed as she rooted in her purse for a scrap of paper and a pen.

Annie's eyes turned back to the twins as the woman wrote out her name and number, still talking about what an amazing job Wally did on the boat's details. Annie decided not to tell her about Emily's contribution of licked popsicle sticks. Somehow, she doubted the trendy young mother would see that as a plus.

A group of five boys, with Annie's grandson, John, in the center, were gathered around the boat. One of the boys held the whale Annie had found in a Stony Point shop and included with John's gift. Clearly the whale was attempting some kind of sneak attack on the lobster boat.

Three of the other boys held the crewmen that Annie had found in the same toy store as the whale. The men were running around the deck in a panic at the approaching whale. Captain John was shouting nautical-sounding orders to the crew as he clutched his captain figure.

Annie was glad her gifts were such a hit. They were all a team effort. She never would have come up with such a wonderful model boat in the shops of Brookfield. The very idea for the boat had come from Ian. She wouldn't have thought to make a doll without her mother's careful saving of Jenny's doll. She wouldn't have managed the lovely sweaters without the help of Kate and Mary Beth.

"Some of the other moms asked about the boat too," the young woman said suddenly, breaking into Annie's thoughts. "Should I collect their names? Do you think your friend could do more than one boat?"

"I think he would like that," Annie said.

"I'm underlining my name though," she said, and then she whispered, "I asked first."

Annie nodded, smiling at the suggestion that she was "calling dibs" on the first boat. Wally would enjoy knowing he was so wildly popular that women in Texas would fight over him. The young woman hurried across the room to a group of other moms.

"You know, I still hate being reminded that you're going back to Stony Point," LeeAnn said as she stepped up beside her mother.

Annie turned to look at her daughter. She had the same fair hair that Annie thought of as a trait of the Holden women. LeeAnn was a bit taller than Annie, but they looked a lot alike, though LeeAnn lacked the sprinkling of gray that ran through Annie's own shoulder-length blond hair. "Stony Point has done a lot for me," Annie said. "I was in a giant holding pattern here after your father died. In Stony Point, I feel like I'm finally starting to heal."

LeeAnn nodded. "I can see it. I could see it when you got off the plane. Your feet don't drag anymore. And your smile doesn't look so sad." She shrugged and turned to look at the children. "But I miss you, Mom. I want the kids to know you as they grow up. I want us to stay close."

"I miss you too," Annie said. "But you know, there is no reason we can't stay close. Now that I've decided where to live, I don't have to hide from Brookfield any more. We can make plans for when I'll visit here, and when you'll bring the children to visit me."

"Mom," LeeAnn said, shaking her head in resignation, "you know what Herb's schedule is like."

Annie nodded. "I knew what your dad's schedule was like too. And I let him work so much that work was our life.

Your dad loved the car lot, and I did too, for his sake. But now ... well, I wish I'd dragged him away to Stony Point now and then. Just be careful that you don't end up with a lot of wishes that can't come true, LeeAnn."

Her daughter nodded. "I'll think about it."

Annie knew she wouldn't get any clearer commitment than that, so she let it drop and turned her eyes back to the children. The two women watched the battle between lobster boat and whale for a moment. Then LeeAnn said, "You certainly made Pastor Mitchell happy. I thought he would explode in church this morning waiting for announcement time to tell everyone about the missionary retreat."

Annie nodded. Just then, John raced over to Annie. He pointed back at the group of other boys. "What kind of whale is that?"

"A fin whale," Annie said, remembering what the shopkeeper had told her. She'd known John would want to know all the facts, so she'd memorized them carefully. "They're the second largest whale in the world, and the largest you're likely to spot off the coast of Maine."

"Do they have teeth?" John asked.

"No," Annie said. "They're called baleen whales because they have a kind of sieve in their mouths called a baleen. It lets them sift tiny bits of food out of the water."

John nodded. "I thought so." He stomped back toward the group, shouting, "It could *not* eat the captain. It doesn't have teeth!"

Annie and LeeAnn laughed. "Maybe I should have bought him some sharks too," Annie said. "You know, the mayor of Stony Point said he'd get his brother to take us on a whale watch when you bring the kids out for a visit. I can check and see what the best times of year are ... "

"You check," LeeAnn said, "but I'm not making any promises. You drove me crazy with wondering for almost a year. I think you can dangle for a few weeks while we work out a holiday schedule."

"That seems fair," Annie said.

"But whenever we do come," LeeAnn said, "no mysteries."

"I can't make any promises about that," Annie said, laughing again. "The mysteries are never my idea. They just happen when I least expect them."

LeeAnn reached out and gave her mother a hug. "Then I'll just have to accept that my mom is a mystery magnet who lives in Maine." She sighed and laid her head on her mother's shoulder. Annie hugged her back, completely and totally happy.

# About The Author

Jan Fields loves trying new needlecrafts from tatting lace to crocheting sweaters for her daughter's dolls. She has designed a variety of soft toys and written articles on toy design. She has written sixteen books for an educational publisher and is working on a science fiction series for teens for the same publisher. Her short fiction and articles have appeared in a variety of magazine publications. When she's not tapping away on her computer keyboard, she enjoys visiting new and interesting places around New England with her family.

*J*oin Annie Dawson and the members of the Hook and Needle Club of Stony Point, Maine, as they track down mysteries connected with the contents found in the attic of Annie's ancestral home, Grey Gables. There will be danger, adventures and heartwarming discoveries in the secrets Annie unearths—secrets about her own family as well as the townspeople of this charming seacoast town in central Maine. Let the good people of Stony Point warm your heart and the mysteries of Annie's Attic keep you on the edge of your seat.

*To find out how to get other books in this series visit* AnniesMysteries.com